THE POWERBROKER

NORCROSS SECURITY #6

ANNA HACKETT

The Powerbroker

Published by Anna Hackett

Copyright 2021 by Anna Hackett

Cover by Lana Pecherczyk

Cover image by Wander Aguiar

Edits by Tanya Saari

ISBN (ebook): 978-1-922414-40-3

ISBN (paperback): 978-1-922414-41-0

Norcross Security out loads of times, and had run interference for them more times than Vander could count.

Running a successful private investigations and security firm kept him busy. Unlike Hunt, who was hampered by the rules, Vander could operate quite happily in the gray.

He did whatever the fuck was necessary to keep his people, his family, and friends safe.

What Hunt was asking him to do was screwed. Put a detective—a female one—undercover with the worst biker gang in San Francisco.

No, it did not sit right with Vander at all.

Suddenly, a figure detached itself from the shadows of a nearby alley. South Beach was filled with renovated warehouses and buildings, like the one Vander gutted to create the Norcross Security office. But if you were looking for the shadows, you could still find them.

"Hey!" The young man brandished a pocketknife. "Give me your wallet and watch."

Vander cocked a brow. The man's voice had a faint Southern twang, and he clearly wasn't from around here. His pale skin was flushed, his red hair mussed, and his pupils were dilated. He was also perspiring. He was high on something. Probably Stardust. There'd been an influx of the synthetic drug lately.

"You don't want to do this," Vander said.

"I said give me your wallet!" Spittle flew from the man's mouth. "And that shiny watch, Mr. Fancy Suit."

Vander was partial to his Omega. Had no plans to hand it over.

He sighed. "You sure you want to do this?"

CHAPTER ONE

Visiting police headquarters was never his favorite thing to do.

Vander Norcross straightened his suit jacket, then strode across the street. His reason for today's visit to the guys and gals in blue had him in a bad mood.

His long stride ate up the sidewalk. Due to the nice, late-spring weather, and the fact that police headquarters was in Mission Bay, right next door to his own office, he'd decided to walk.

Hopefully, he could shake his sense of impending doom before he got there.

His years in the military—many of those leading a covert Ghost Ops team on dangerous, impossible missions—had taught him to never ignore his instincts.

That got you killed, fast.

He was due to meet with his friend Detective Hunter "Hunt" Morgan in fifteen minutes. Vander knew he owed his friend several times over. Hunt had helped

At Star's End – One of Library Journal's Best E-Original Romances for 2014

The Phoenix Adventures – SFR Galaxy Award Winner for Most Fun New Series and "Why Isn't This a Movie?" Series

Beneath a Trojan Moon – SFR Galaxy Award Winner and RWAus Ella Award Winner

Hell Squad – SFR Galaxy Award for best Post-Apocalypse for Readers who don't like Post-Apocalypse

"Like Indiana Jones meets Star Wars. A treasure hunt with a steamy romance." – SFF Dragon, review of *Among Galactic Ruins*

"Action, danger, aliens, romance – yup, it's another great book from Anna Hackett!" – Book Gannet Reviews, review of *Hell Squad: Marcus*

Sign up for my VIP mailing list and get your *free box set* containing three action-packed romances.

Visit here to get started: www.annahackett.com

WHAT READERS ARE SAYING ABOUT ANNA'S ACTION ROMANCE

Heart of Eon - Romantic Book of the Year (Ruby) winner 2020

Cyborg - PRISM Award Winner 2019

Edge of Eon and Mission: Her Protection - Romantic Book of the Year (Ruby) finalists 2019

Unfathomed and Unmapped - Romantic Book of the Year (Ruby) finalists 2018

Unexplored – Romantic Book of the Year (Ruby) Novella Winner 2017

Return to Dark Earth – One of Library Journal's Best E-Original Books for 2015 and two-time SFR Galaxy Awards winner

"I'll stick you! Shut up, and hand them over."

Vander moved.

His first hit was to the man's arm, and his would-be attacker dropped his knife with a sharp cry. Vander spun, and followed up with a quick elbow to the face. The guy cried out again and Vander kicked his legs out from under him. The man fell heavily to the sidewalk and let out a strangled groan.

Vander pressed his boot to the man's back, and picked up the pocketknife. Then he yanked some zip ties from his jacket pocket and trussed the man's wrists and ankles together.

"You're not from around here, so I took it easy on you."

The man flopped like a fish. "What the fuck? What the fuck!"

Vander crouched. "My name's Vander Norcross."

The young man froze, fear seeping into his eyes.

"Oh, so you have heard of me." Vander leaned closer and lowered his voice. "This is my turf. I don't like innocent people getting attacked and mugged by junkies."

"I-I-I—"

"Won't do it again." Vander lowered his voice to icy levels. "If I hear you're approaching anyone, I'll find out and I'll make you regret it." He gave the man an icy half smile. "I'm good at finding people. You get me?"

The man nodded rapidly.

"Good." Vander rose.

"...ah, you going to untie me?"

"No." Vander started walking away.

"Hey, what about my knife?"

3

"I'm keeping it."

Vander strode away and crossed the bridge over Mission Bay. Soon, he spotted the Public Safety Building complex that housed the San Francisco Police Department headquarters, along with the local fire station and arson team.

He entered the police station and checked in at reception. He also handed in the knife and reported his Southern friend.

The cop behind the glass rolled her eyes. "Is he bleeding, Norcross?"

"Please. I can take down a hopped-up junkie without bloodshed, Officer Cortez. He wasn't even bruised."

The woman grinned. "You can take me down anytime you like."

Vander smiled at her. "That big, ex-footballer husband of yours might not be happy about that."

Officer Cortez sighed. "True. Go through. You know the way."

Vander navigated the corridors and headed up to where Hunt and the other detectives had their offices. The building was all concrete and glass, and very modern.

He passed a crying woman with mascara running down her face, who was being consoled by a detective. The background soundtrack was ringing phones and murmured conversations. It was a far cry from being in the military. Hunt had been Delta Force, until an injury had forced him to retire.

Vander had left Ghost Ops before he'd had to. The military would've kept him. He'd been good at killing, and good at keeping his men alive in the shittiest of circumstances. His heart thumped hard once. Not all of them, though. Some had never come home.

He'd seen things that the crying woman behind him couldn't even imagine in her worst nightmares.

He reached Hunt's office. The detective was standing, talking on the phone.

"Yes, I need it impounded. Yes, I needed it done yesterday." Hunt spotted Vander and waved him in.

The office was small and neat. Hunt wasn't one for many trinkets, and he wasn't married, so no photos of a pretty wife and kids. There was a framed picture of him with his two brothers. Ryder, a paramedic, who patched up the Norcross guys on occasion. He also donated his time at a free clinic in the Tenderloin. Camden was also Ghost Ops, and about to get out. Vander had offered him a job at Norcross.

Hunt hung up the phone. "Hi, Vander."

"Hunt."

The detective kept in shape. Leaving Delta Force hadn't softened him. His light-brown hair was cut short, and his eyes were a deep green. He circled the desk and leaned against it. "You're still unhappy about this."

Vander cocked a brow. "About you railroading me into putting an unknown woman in a dangerous position with a motorcycle club? Yes."

"She's not a woman, she's a detective. A good one. And she's on her way, so she won't be unknown for long."

Vander grunted. He wandered over to one of the shelves. Hunt had a glass paperweight made to look like a police badge. Cute. Vander lifted it. "If she's experienced, Trucker might know who she is."

Trucker Patterson was the head of the Iron Wanderers MC. He was an all-around asshole, but Vander kept lines of communication open with the man. It let Trucker know that Vander was watching him.

The Wanderers kept a pretty public-friendly face, with a clubhouse and garage out in Oakland. Not all the members were assholes. Some just liked the lifestyle—bikes, riding, parties, living free. But behind the scenes, there were some who were involved in illegal shit—usually drugs and weapons. There were plenty of law-abiding motorcycle clubs around; the Iron Wanderers wasn't one of them.

"Sullivan hasn't been a detective long," Hunt said.

Vander groaned. "A newbie? You're fucking kidding me, Hunt. How many undercover assignments has she done?"

Hunt held up a hand. "Hear me out, she's new but good. This is her third undercover assignment."

Vander bit out a curse.

"As the *lead*," Hunt continued. "She's been on other undercover assignments as part of the team. She's solid, Vander."

"Hunt, this is a fucking bad idea. Sending a female, an inexperienced one, at that, into the Wanderers' clubhouse is like sending a lamb to the slaughter."

"*Baaaa*," an amused voice said from the doorway. "The difference is this lamb is trained and armed."

Vander snapped his head around. He didn't drop the paperweight, but damned if his pulse didn't spike.

He didn't like it. He'd learned years ago to control his emotions. When you were standing in the back of a Blackhawk, waiting to fast rope into hell, you learned to keep all your reactions and emotions under control.

Control was something Vander practiced in all aspects of his life.

"Vander Norcross," Hunt said, "Detective Brynn Sullivan."

She smiled. She had thick, brown hair, but brown was totally the wrong word to describe it. There were many different shades in it, from caramel to chocolate, and it was pulled back in a sleek ponytail. She wore black, fitted pants, and a pale blue shirt tucked into them. On her belt was a holstered SIG Sauer and her badge.

She was medium height, with a fit body, and sharp eyes the color of her shirt. She studied him steadily, meeting his gaze straight on.

Vander realized then how few people did that.

She held out her hand. "I'd say it's a pleasure, but we both know I'd be lying. You think I'm, what was it? Female and inexperienced, and I've heard *all* about you."

Vander shook her hand. Her grip was firm, her fingernails natural and cut short. This close to her, he saw she had an intriguing sprinkle of freckles across her nose.

"Really?" he said.

Brynn Sullivan stepped back. "Dangerous, with a blatant disregard for the law."

Hunt made a choked sound.

Vander didn't take his gaze off her. He raised a brow. "I think blatant is a bit much. I respect the law."

"Except when it gets in your way?" she challenged.

"Detective, I don't let *anything* get in my way."

―――――――――

VANDER NORCROSS WAS SO MUCH MORE than she'd expected.

Brynn Sullivan kept her face carefully neutral. With two nosy sisters and one overprotective brother, she'd had lots of practice.

Norcross had a big, muscular body that looked far too good in a suit. His military background was clear in the way he held himself. A predator ready to explode into action when required. She knew his history. He'd been a Ghost Ops commander—in charge of a team of the toughest, hardest, most skilled soldiers in the military. She knew the reputation of Norcross Security, as well.

But no one had warned her about the handsome, rugged face, the bronze skin, or the black eyes.

Or the dangerous vibe that emanated off him.

Dangerous in a "I can and I will take you down" kind of way, and dangerous to any woman brave enough to tangle with him.

She realized suddenly that his eyes weren't black—they were deep, dark blue.

Brynn refused to be intimidated. Her detective badge wasn't very old, but she was damn good at her job. "So, how about we discuss the Iron Wanderers MC? And when you'll make my introduction with Trucker Patterson?"

Norcross just continued to stare at her and she stared

back. If a few knots formed in her belly, she refused to let them show.

"Sit down, Vander," Hunt said.

Vander didn't move for a beat, then he dropped into a chair.

Brynn took the one beside him. She got a faint whisper of his aftershave—fresh and crisp with a darker undertone. It made her think of dark ocean waters.

"Again, I urge you away from this course of action," Norcross said.

"No." Brynn leaned forward. "We've tracked an increase in Stardust—aka bath salts aka synthetic cathinones—on the streets to the Wanderers."

Norcross scowled. "Trucker wouldn't do that. He knows to stick to his turf."

"Or you'll make him regret it?" she asked.

He caught her gaze. "Yes."

Brynn didn't completely disagree with how Norcross operated. She knew Hunt felt the same, which was why he worked with Norcross, and often smoothed things over with the chief and the rest of the brass.

But Brynn knew that when you bent the rules too often, eventually you were tempted to break them. If you dipped your toe in the muck too many times, eventually it clung. She'd seen it happen.

Because of that, her father was dead.

Her stomach hardened. Norcross was her way into the Iron Wanderers. That was all Brynn cared about.

This was her first big case, and she had plenty to prove.

She wasn't going to screw it up.

"Trucker is probably sticking to the agreement in principle," Hunt said. "An out-of-towner has muscled in. They have something over Trucker, don't know what. Trucker is turning a blind eye, and letting the new player deal Stardust in San Francisco."

Norcross frowned. "How do you know this?"

"We have an informant in the Wanderers," Brynn said. "They get me intel when they can, but they're low level. I need more, so I need in there myself."

"These are not nice guys," Vander said. "Women are second-class citizens to most of them."

She lifted her chin. "I can take care of myself. I'm not planning to sign up for life."

"We heard Trucker needs a new supplier of parts for the bike business," Hunt said.

Vander nodded. "He's been bitching about it for ages."

"You'll introduce Brynn as a reliable supplier."

Norcross' dark brows rose. "You'll be undercover as—"

"A mechanic with a sideline in excellent parts, from shady parts unknown," she said.

"Trucker will never buy that." Norcross' gaze skated down her body. "You look and smell like a cop."

His perusal ignited tingles that annoyed her. "Yes, he will buy it. Your job is the introduction, Norcross. Dealing with Trucker is mine." She crossed her arms over her chest.

His jaw tightened. It was a hell of a jaw—strong, covered in dark stubble. Then his gaze narrowed on her face for a second before it flicked to Hunt.

"You two are related. She has your nose, and the same stubborn look you get when you're pissed."

"Cousin," Hunt said.

Brynn smiled. "Although he sometimes likes to treat me like a little sister."

"I only have brothers, so..." Hunt shrugged one broad shoulder.

"You really want to send your cousin into Trucker's lair?" Norcross asked.

"No, I want to send a competent detective in to do her job."

"And save lives," Brynn added. "We need to identify and stop this new supplier. Stop kids from overdosing on Stardust."

Brynn thought back to the crime scene from the night before. She'd spent hours there, and even now, she could still see the cold, dead bodies of the two boys who'd ODed.

No more dead kids. She'd vowed it.

Vander released a breath and stood in one lithe move.

And dammit if she didn't notice how he moved. She straightened. She wasn't here to notice anything about Vander Norcross. She needed his connection to Trucker, that was it.

"Fine," Vander said. "I'll set things in motion with Trucker. Meet me at my office tonight so we can go over the plan. I'll assume you'll want to come after hours so no one spots you."

She nodded. "No one will see me if I don't want them to."

He gave her one more piercing look. "Detective Sullivan." He sent a chin lift in Hunt's direction and then strode out.

Brynn barely suppressed the need to release a breath. "Well, your friend is rather intense."

"Yes, but he knows his stuff. We can trust him."

She wrinkled her nose. "You sure? He strikes me as a man who will do whatever he needs to in order to achieve his own goals."

"He's a good man, Brynn. I trust him with my life. I'm trusting him with yours."

Brynn rose and elbowed her cousin in the side. "Well, I'm heading out to meet an informant." And later, she needed to prep her cover.

Hunt grabbed her arm. "You be careful. If you need backup, or you get a bad vibe, or you get a sniff of things going bad, you call for help."

Brynn kissed his cheek. "Thanks, Hunt."

"Go. Tell that brother of yours he owes me a beer."

"Will do."

"I still haven't forgiven him for bucking the family trend to become a smoke eater."

Brynn rolled her eyes. It was a familiar complaint. Both her father and Hunt's father had been cops and best friends. Her father had married Hunt's father's sister. Her brother, Bard, had been copping the brunt of family teasing ever since he'd joined the fire department.

"Bye." Brynn stopped by her desk and shrugged her jacket on, then grabbed her bag.

As she headed out, she saw two female cops chatting.

"You missed seeing that prime hunk of lickable hotness."

"Damn. Vander Norcross might scare the bejesus out of me, but that man's ass... Mmm-hmm."

"I know, right. If he crooked his finger my way, I'd run as fast as I could and shed my clothes on the way."

Brynn's jaw tightened.

"Girl, I think that Vander Norcross is more the kind of man to tear a woman's clothes off."

Both women sighed.

Brynn kept walking.

Objectively, she knew that the man was hot. His Italian-American, dark good looks, his body, the dangerous vibe. It was a hell of a combination.

Shame he could also be dangerous and reckless. She shook her head and headed out.

Her phone rang and she yanked it out, then pulled a face. It was her older, bossy sister, Naomi. Nay was sure she'd been born to rule the world. She employed her enviable skills on five-year-olds as a teacher.

Her sister's face popped up on the screen.

"Hi, Nay," Brynn said.

"Hey, Sis." Naomi looked like a younger version of their mom, and had dark brown hair cut in a neat bob that was always blow-dried with precision. "You look like a woman on a mission."

"Always," Brynn replied.

Naomi took a breath. "Soooo..."

Nothing good ever happened when her sister started off with a drawn-out so. "No."

Naomi pulled a face. "Let me ask first. There's this great guy at work I want to set you up with."

"No."

"At least give it—"

"No."

Naomi huffed. "Jack is nice."

"Then definitely no."

"Argh, you are so stubborn and single-minded, Brynn."

"I have no time for men or dating." A dark, rugged face flashed in her head, and she quickly snuffed it out. "But I still love you for trying to set me up at least once a month." Even when it drove Brynn crazy.

Naomi took her role as oldest sister seriously, and since she'd gotten engaged to her teacher fiancé, Brian, she was determined to see her siblings married as well.

Another huff from her sister. "I love you too, even when you aggravate me, and I worry you'll die alone, clutching your gun."

Brynn smiled. "I like my gun. Now, I have to go. I've got a big case, and lots of prep work to do."

Naomi shook her head. "It's always work with you."

"Always. See you at Mom's place for dinner next week."

Brynn had barely gone two steps when her phone signaled another video call. She rolled her eyes. It was her younger sister, Carrin. "God, Naomi was fast."

Carrin grinned. "She knew you'd say no and had me lined up." The much blonder, short-haired Carrin—who worked as an attorney—schooled her face into a serious look. "Brynn, go out with Naomi's nice, boring friend."

"No, you go out with him."

"I'm banging that assistant DA, so she's not hassling me."

Brynn thought for a second. "That one with the square jaw and the nice ass?"

"That's him. We're friends with benefits and it works for me."

"Don't rub it in," Brynn said. "You've done your duty. Go."

Carrin waved and winked off.

A second later, Brynn's phone rang. She growled and considered throwing it at the wall, until she saw it was her mom.

She pressed it to her ear. "Hi, Mom. And no, I'm not going on a date with Naomi's friend, Jack."

"Hi, darling girl. He sounds very nice."

"I'm not interested, and I'm busy. I have a big case."

"Stubborn and dedicated. Just like your father." That familiar tone held a blend of both old grief and love.

Brynn's belly locked. God, she really missed her dad. She wished she could sit with him, have a beer, ask him advice. "I take that as a compliment."

"I know. All right, sweetie, I'll let you go. See you later."

"Bye, Mom." Brynn was tight with her family, and loved them all to pieces, even when sometimes she wished they lived a little farther away.

Her phone vibrated. It was a text from Bard.

Naomi keeps texting me about some guy named Jack.

She wants me to have sex with him.

Not going anywhere near that! Why don't you agree to dinner with this guy?

I don't have time. You go out with him then.

Is he gay?

I don't think so.

Not my type then.

Bard was currently single. His last boyfriend had been a hunky ER nurse. Like Brynn, he didn't have much time for dating or relationships.

I have a work thing later, but I'll see you tonight.

I'm cooking, so don't worry about dinner.

Finally, some good news. Firefighters all had to cook when they were at the station, so Bard was pretty decent in the kitchen. Brynn finally shoved her phone into her pocket and strode down the corridor.

Naomi meant well, but right now, Brynn didn't have time for men. Maybe one day, in the distant future. If she found the right one—someone strong, tough, loyal, trustworthy. Oh, and a nice jaw and ass wouldn't go astray.

No, first, she had a plan to prove herself as a new detective.

To herself.

To the memory of her dad.

That's the one thing she and Vander Norcross had in common: not letting anything get in their way.

CHAPTER TWO

B rynn rushed around her apartment. She'd gotten in late from work, and was now late to meet Norcross.

Luckily, she lived on the border between South Beach and Mission Bay. Her place wasn't fancy, but it did the job. She shared it with Bard. It was in a good building with amenities, and close to the Public Safety Building, and that worked well for both of them.

They hardly ever saw each other since they both worked lots of hours.

Brynn changed out of her pantsuit. If anyone saw her near the Norcross office, she didn't want to look like a cop. She pulled on dark jeans and her favorite drab-olive T-shirt. Next, she pulled on her cap for her favorite hockey team—the San Jose Sharks. Whenever she could, she caught some of their home games.

She headed out the door and hustled toward the Norcross office. It would be easier to walk than drive.

If Norcross could make the introduction to the Iron Wanderers tomorrow, she could finally make some headway on this case. She'd been late because not only had she arrested a guy on another case, she'd been at the autopsy of a teen who'd ODed on Stardust a few days ago. The parents were distraught. The girl had been a top student, never done any drugs before, and went to a party... Now her life was over.

These drugs were stronger, and laced with crap like cleaning fluids. Brynn let out a breath. Her father had been a good cop. All her life, all she'd ever wanted was to be a cop like him, and help people.

She turned onto the street where the Norcross Security office was located and saw it ahead.

Nice. Clearly, private security and investigations paid well. She'd heard rumors that Norcross and his men cost a pretty penny.

The brick of the warehouse was complemented with lots of glass and black metal. Whoever had done the conversion had done good work. She discreetly scanned her surroundings. No one on the street was paying her any special attention. She pressed the intercom button by the front door.

A second later, the door beeped and unlocked.

She strode inside, tugging her cap off. The industrial, modern vibe continued. It was an open plan in the center, with wooden beams and metal ductwork overhead. Glass-walled offices lined each side of the space. The place was empty this late at night.

"Good evening."

That wasn't Norcross' voice. She spun.

She discovered a golden god in a tuxedo. She knew who he was instantly. She'd read up on all of them. Saxon

Buchanan was Vander's best friend and right-hand man. He was also engaged to Vander's sister, Gia.

"Hey," Brynn said.

Green eyes took her in. It would be easy to dismiss him as a handsome man with money, but she knew he was former Ghost Ops as well, and she saw the alert way he watched her.

"I was just heading out. He's waiting for you." Saxon cocked his head. "You don't look like a cop."

Brynn lifted a brow. "And you don't look like a badass. Looks can be deceiving."

His lips quirked. "Touché."

"So, you think I don't look like a cop because I'm a woman?"

Buchanan shook his head. "Because you don't have that jaded, resigned look in your eye."

"I know better than to try and save everyone." Her dad had taught her that. "But I can save a few."

Saxon Buchanan's lips twitched. "Good motto. That said, Trucker and the Wanderers will chew you up and spit you out."

"You don't know anything about me, Buchanan." She strolled closer and winked. "One thing is that I'm tough. They try to chew on me, they'll choke."

Now, his lips moved into a full smile. "I hope you're right." With a nod, he headed for the stairs to the lower level.

Brynn wandered deeper into the office, following the light on at the end of the row of offices. She moved to a doorway. This office didn't have glass walls like the others.

The domain of the boss.

A modern, metal lamp was on by the desk, but the rest of the room was shadowed. Vander wasn't sitting at the desk.

"Detective."

The deep voice from the shadows to the right made her spin. He was cloaked in darkness, but she knew instantly that it was him. Damn, she hadn't even been able to tell he was there.

"Evening, Norcross."

"I expected you earlier."

She shrugged. "I had another case run late."

Vander stepped forward and her heart did a little pitty-pat. *Dammit.* The man was way too much for any woman's system.

"Did you get your guy?" he asked.

She smiled. "Yep. He's sitting in a comfy cell waiting for arraignment." She scanned around. "I like your place."

"Thanks." He waved toward the chairs in front of his glossy desk. It was all very slick. He probably thought the sleek lines and lack of personal touches didn't say anything about him.

But she was good at reading between the lines, and she thought it said a lot. She sat.

"I traded calls with Trucker," Norcross said. "We've set up a meeting for tomorrow."

Brynn straightened, her pulse spiking. "That's great."

Norcross leaned against his desk. "You haven't changed your mind about this?"

Her gaze narrowed. "No."

He crossed his arms over his chest. He wasn't wearing a jacket, and his sleeves were rolled up. Her belly coiled. What was it about a man's forearms that were so damn sexy when his sleeves were rolled up?

"Fine. I told Hunt I owed him, so I'll follow through. You get yourself killed, it's not my problem."

She smiled sweetly. "No, it isn't."

"Any idea who this out-of-towner is?"

She shook her head. "No. They're laying low. My contact in the club doesn't know who they are. They've had a few new members join recently."

"I highly doubt your informant is a club member, so I'm guessing it's one of the women."

"I don't give up my informants, Norcross."

"You might need backup in there."

"Like I said, I can take care of myself."

His mouth flattened. "These guys aren't nice. They don't respect women. They won't treat you like a lady."

Brynn rose and moved toward him. "This isn't my first rodeo. I know exactly what to expect."

He pushed off the desk and rose to meet her. The toes of his shoes bumped hers.

"Have you got a problem with women being cops?" Was he just another chauvinist?

"No, I just don't like seeing women hurt."

His tone made her want to shiver. The darkness in his eyes made her belly tie up in knots. What horrors had he seen?

And why did she feel the crazy urge to try and comfort him?

She stepped back. "I appreciate your concern. Now, the meet?"

He stared at her for a beat, then circled his desk and sat in his chair. "I'm meeting with Trucker at the club-house tomorrow at two PM. It's in Oakland—"

"I know where it is."

"Good. Arrive at 2:10 and I'll make the introduc-tion." His gaze drifted down her clothes. "Sure you can pull off biker?"

"Yes. Don't worry."

"Oh, I'll worry."

Brynn's gaze drifted over his desk, and she noticed his computer monitor was on. A hockey game was playing in the lower corner.

"Hey, the Sharks game." She leaned closer. "I think they could go all the way this season."

He shifted closer and she got another hit of his cologne. Ugh, she wished he didn't have to smell so good. She was a sucker for a sexy cologne.

"Yeah," he said. "With Jackson as wing, they're looking good, but they're behind."

"Ross is excellent in defense. They'll claw back."

He cocked his head. "You're a hockey fan?"

She tilted her cap so he could see the logo on it. "Hockey makes life worth living, Norcross. But baseball and football aren't bad either."

The corner of his lips curled. Not quite a smile, but still devastating. What would it feel like to have Vander Norcross really smile at you?

Her chest tightened. *No.* He was a means to an end. A dangerous one she couldn't afford to tangle with.

22

"Looks like you have a redeeming feature after all, Detective Sullivan."

She straightened and pulled her cap on. "Don't worry, Norcross. I'm sure my other annoying traits will remind you that you don't like me."

He turned to face her. "I never said I didn't like you."

Her gaze met his. It was dark, cool, and made her think of glass. Yes, Norcross wore that cool, aloof façade well, but the detective in her sensed the contained violence underneath. *Shit.* She'd never been attracted to dangerous men before. She wasn't starting now.

"I'm a cop. I like rules, law, and order. I'm not sure you do."

"We need rules, Detective, but sometimes those rules get so tight, that the bad guys get away with bad things. That, I can't live with."

She cocked her head. "I'm the one to uphold the law, not you."

"We each have our role to play."

Grr. She wanted to argue with him. Anyone who thought they could take the law into their own hands would eventually make a bad choice. Like her father's partner had.

She reined in her temper. She needed Norcross for now.

"So, I'll see you tomorrow." Her tone was admirably even.

Vander inclined his head. "Tomorrow."

Brynn strode out and forced herself not to look back. *Focus on the job, Sullivan.*

She had to pull off this cover perfectly. She had a lot riding on this.

THIS WAS A FUCKING BAD IDEA.

It went against every instinct he had. Vander rode his BMW S1000RR motorcycle across the Bay Bridge toward Oakland. The Iron Wanderers had set up the clubhouse in the Hoover-Foster neighborhood.

They had a garage for bike storage and restoration, and customizations, and a gated clubhouse next door in an old, ugly, concrete building with few windows. Inside, they had a bar, darts, pool tables, and out back, a fight ring.

It got loud and messy when they partied.

He pulled up out front. The garage had three bays, and two of the large doors were open. He swung off his bike and Trucker wandered out, wiping his hands on a rag.

Trucker was a big guy with a head of thick, salt-and-pepper hair, a trim beard, and a gut that was going a little soft.

He eyed Vander's bike. "We need to get you on a Harley, Norcross."

"My ride's just fine."

Trucker grunted and shoved his hands in the pockets of his dirty jeans.

"When I needed a new parts supplier, didn't expect you to help solve my problem." Trucker sucked and spat on the sidewalk. "We don't always see eye to eye."

"You don't piss me off, Trucker, then we have no beef. And if you help me, I'll help you."

Trucker sniffed. "You say this guy of yours can supply quality parts for the agreed prices?"

"She can."

"She?" Trucker's bushy brows winged up.

Yeah, Trucker was old school, believing a woman's rightful place was flat on her back with her legs spread. Another reason Vander didn't want Detective Brynn Sullivan anywhere near the Wanderers.

"Yes, she. She's good, and she can take care of herself." Vander hoped.

Trucker grinned. "Plus, she has San Francisco's biggest motherfucker at her back."

Vander didn't respond, just maintained eye contact until Trucker's muddy-brown gaze skittered away.

There was a throaty roar of an engine. Vander turned his head, and he and Trucker watched a sleek, gleaming Triumph zip down the street.

There was a slim, helmeted rider on top of it.

The bike pulled up in the driveway of the garage, right in front of them. Vander's chest locked.

"Well, fuck me," Trucker said.

The bike's rider wore a tiny pair of denim shorts, showing off a lot of sleek leg. Where the hell had she been hiding those long legs?

She pulled the black helmet off and caramel-brown hair fell everywhere.

Brynn shot him a smug grin. Next, she pulled on her well-worn San Jose Sharks hockey cap, and tugged her hair out the hole at the back.

Vander blinked. Her tiny, checked shirt had enough buttons open to show more than a hint of cleavage. She also had tattoos running up her left arm in an explosion of color that hadn't been there yesterday—it looked like a tangle of rose vines. He knew they were fake, but they looked real.

She swung those long legs over the bike to stand. She was wearing a pair of cowboy boots.

"Howdy, boys."

Her accent was subtly different. Not as polished and clipped as when he'd first met her.

"Well, hello there," Trucker drawled.

Vander turned to stare at the man.

When Trucker glanced his way, his smile slipped and he cleared his throat.

"Hey, V." Brynn winked at him, then she turned to Trucker. "You must be the president of the Iron Wanderers." She stuck out her hand. "I'm Bry Davis."

"Trucker." He shook her hand. "What's Bry short for, beautiful?"

Her smile turned a little mean. "None of your business. Now, how about we talk parts?" She stepped up to the open door of the garage and scanned inside. "Looks like you've got a decent setup." She crossed her arms. "I will warn you, my parts are in demand."

"I bet." Trucker eyed her legs.

Vander swiveled. One more fucking comment, and he was dragging her long legs out of there.

Trucker's mouth firmed. "Right. Let's talk business."

The biker led Brynn inside, leaving Vander to follow behind.

He'd been in the clubhouse a few times, and usually found it a mass of empty beer bottles and other detritus, but it looked like the Wanderers took the custom-bike business more seriously. The garage was well organized, with tools all stacked neatly in place. It was their legitimate business, while behind-the-scenes, they ran the illegal fight nights and dealt drugs.

"So, we need a steady supply of parts." Trucker rambled on.

Brynn paused every now and then, and asked some questions. She sure as hell sounded like she knew what she was talking about.

Vander found himself equal parts intrigued and annoyed. If she hadn't known her stuff, he could've walked her out of there and sent her back safely to police headquarters.

Instead, she had Trucker eating out of the palm of her hand. A few times, the biker even laughed.

As she answered questions, Vander saw she was grudgingly gaining the biker's respect.

As Brynn leaned over to study a half-built bike, Vander's gaze dropped.

Fuck. Those damn legs were on display and her tiny denim shorts hugged her sweet ass.

She straightened and Vander scowled.

He had zero business noticing Brynn's—Detective Sullivan's—assets. She was Hunt's cousin. And a cop.

Plus she was trouble. Smart, opinionated women were always trouble. He should know—he had one for a sister.

He kept his life uncomplicated and trouble-free. If he

felt like a fuck, he fucked, and that was it. He ensured his partner for the night enjoyed herself, and he left.

"You run a tight ship, Trucker," Brynn said.

"Yeah, darlin'. We like to have a good time, but we take care of business, too."

Brynn's smile was wide and sassy. "I've heard that about bikers. How many in your club?"

Jeez, she was flirting and pumping Trucker for information.

Okay, Vander was more than a little turned on, and it really annoyed the hell out of him.

"I can get your parts." As Brynn turned, her brown ponytail bobbed. She rested her hands on her hips, and that made the ink on her left arm stick out. It looked so real. "For the right price."

Vander listened to them haggle. Unsurprisingly, she was good at it.

"So, do we have a deal?" she asked Trucker.

"We do, darlin'." Trucker held out a beefy hand.

The pair shook.

"Thanks for hooking me up, V." She shot Vander a smile.

He grunted.

"He's always so chatty," she said to Trucker.

The biker made a choked sound, then cleared his throat. "Look, we're having a little party tonight at the clubhouse. It's Friday night and we've got a few new members, so it's a bit of a welcome party. There'll be drinks and food, and some fights in our ring."

Vander stiffened, but Brynn smiled.

"Sounds fun," she said.

"Come, and I'll introduce you around."

"Thanks, Trucker."

The biker's grin dimmed. "You're welcome, too, Norcross."

Vander lifted his chin. He'd been invited before, but he'd never come.

"I'll walk you out," Trucker said.

Vander took Brynn's elbow. "I've got it from here."

She smiled at the biker. "See you tonight."

As they stepped outside, and out of view of Trucker, she tried to pull her elbow free, but Vander held tight. Time for a little conversation.

CHAPTER THREE

Norcross kept a tight hold on her elbow as he marched her out to her bike.

When they got close, Brynn finally pulled her arm free, only for Norcross to pin her against her Triumph.

"Norcross—" He was so damn big, radiating strength.

"You think it's a good idea to flirt with Trucker, and parade around in those clothes?"

She narrowed her gaze. His face was blank, cool, and some crazy part of her wanted to see that ice shatter.

Crap, head in the game, Brynn. "I'm playing my part," she whisper-yelled. "He'll see what I need him to see. It's my job."

She saw a muscle tick in Vander's jaw. It was such a small tell that she almost missed it.

Hmm, not quite so cool after all. And of course, he smelled good. The ones you couldn't have always did.

"Back up, Norcross." She pressed her hands to his chest, covered in his white shirt. Then she was totally distracted by the firm muscles under the cotton. She wondered if that sexy bronze skin covered all of him.

Shit. She forced herself to look up. She was *not* imagining Vander Norcross naked.

Okay, now she was totally picturing him naked.

"Are you listening to me?" he growled.

"No. I figured you were lecturing me, so I could just skip it."

He sucked in a breath, but that face that was a little too tough to be truly handsome—which unfortunately made him more attractive—stayed impassive.

"Not used to people who don't hop to obey your orders?" she asked.

"Not used to people who don't listen to good advice."

"I know what I'm doing."

"The Wanderers' party nights get rough and wild. Their fights, they're bareknuckle."

She leaned in. Anyone watching would see two people having an intense discussion. "I'm a cop, Norcross. Believe me, I know better than most that the world isn't all sunshine and rainbows."

"You have no fucking clue."

She saw the quick flash of shadows in his eyes, and had the insane urge to cup his cheek.

Jeez. She needed to get her head examined. "I do have a clue, here on my streets."

His eyebrows went up. "Your streets?"

She lifted her chin. "Yes."

"My streets. My city."

"Yes, you know everybody, don't you? Vander Norcross, the powerbroker with contacts everywhere.

31

Both good, bad, and very ugly. You're friends with cops and business leaders, friends with gang leaders, mafia, bikers. You know, if you play in the muck with the bad guys long enough, you'll be tempted to take a little for yourself."

"You don't know me." He leaned even closer. "I've spent my life fighting for this country and keeping my people safe. What I want is to keep on ensuring their safety so they never have to deal with the bad guys."

"Like I've said before, that's my job."

He shook his head and gripped her hips. "You'll just have to share."

Her damn pulse went haywire. "Back up, Norcross."

"You're *not* going to that party."

"Sorry, Dad, you can't ground me. The party gives me a chance to get the lay of the land and meet all the players. I might even be able to identify the new guy."

She saw a vein pulsing in his temple. Wow, he was really ticked. "Does everyone do what you say?"

"Pretty much. Except my mom."

Oh, God. There was nothing sexier than a badass who loved his mom.

"Well, this will be character building for you, since I won't follow your orders, either."

He cocked his head, his intense gaze running over her face. She felt his fingers dig into her hips.

For a strange moment, everything seemed magnified —the hard feel of his body, the masculine, ocean scent of him, the warmth of the sun on her skin, the pounding of her heart.

"Back up now," she whispered.

Instead, he stepped closer, and their bodies pressed together. "I'm not sure I want to. I find you intriguing, Detective, when you aren't annoying the hell out of me."

She tilted her head. "You'll find it very intriguing when I plant my fist in your gut."

He smiled. A real, full-on smile.

Holy cow. It should be labeled a deadly weapon. It made that dark, dangerous face outright handsome. Embarrassingly, her panties went damp.

"You could try," he murmured.

She narrowed her gaze. "I could take you, Norcross."

"No, you couldn't." His fingers squeezed her hips, then he stepped back. "Luckily for you, I don't socialize with cops. Your cousin is the exception."

"Worried about what we might dig up?"

Now that he'd stepped away, she almost swayed, missing the feel of him.

God, Brynn.

"No, I just can do without the self-righteous nagging," he said.

She rolled her eyes. "You mean, someone holding you to account."

He looked up. "Are you going to the party?"

She nodded. "I'll do my job."

He stared at her for a beat, then nodded. He walked over to his very sleek, very hot motorcycle. *That was it? No more demands? No fight?*

Brynn felt vaguely disappointed.

He straddled the bike and her mind headed for the gutter. He grabbed his helmet and glanced her way. "Be careful."

She straddled her own bike. "I always am, Norcross. Some of us follow the rules, and weigh the odds."

He sat there, waiting and watching. She realized he was waiting for her to leave first. Gentleman or control freak?

Possibly a bit of both.

Vander Norcross struck her as the kind of man who needed to control everything.

She shot him a look, then traded her cap for her helmet. She started her engine, gunned it, and pulled away.

At the end of the street, she glanced back and saw him riding behind her. He rode his powerful bike with an ease that made her breath catch.

Keep your head on your investigation, Brynn.

Her pulse wasn't as level as she liked.

He rolled up and stopped beside her. She could almost feel the weight of his gaze through the dark visor of his helmet.

The powerful throb of the engine beneath her vibrated through her body. She couldn't see through the dark visor, but she knew he was looking at her.

She leaned forward and took off.

He kept pace right behind her as they rode through traffic and onto the Bay Bridge.

Brynn didn't get to take her bike out as often as she liked. She loved the sense of speed and freedom. She grinned. Damn, it felt good.

And the hot guy on the bike beside her was exhilarating as well.

They zipped across the bridge and as she turned, Vander sent her a salute, then sped away.

Oh, boy. It was going to be extremely challenging to keep her eyes on her case and not on Vander Norcross' mighty fine body. He should be listed as a lethal weapon.

Right, she needed to get her head in the game. She had a biker party to prep for.

VANDER PULLED the X6 to a stop on the crowded street outside the Wanderers clubhouse. There were cars everywhere, and a line of bikes in front of the garage. He climbed out of the SUV. The beat of the music vibrated through the air.

As he approached the open iron gates, he heard the rumble of conversation, punctuated by bouts of raucous laughter.

He wondered if Brynn was there, yet.

Two biker enforcers stood at the gate and watched him coming. They both stiffened and jerked their chins up.

"Norcross," one rumbled.

Vander strode past them. The place was packed with bikers in denim and leather, and women wearing a lot less—short and tight seemed to be the theme.

He watched a biker lift a laughing woman with big hair off her feet. Her beer spilled everywhere.

It was still early, but the night would get a lot rowdier and wilder in the clubhouse. He walked inside and scanned the long bar with flags decorating the wall behind it. They were doing a brisk business.

There was also a sprinkle of the general public here. They enjoyed the party atmosphere.

Large, sliding doors were pushed open to a crowded outdoor area. A grill was being manned, and the smell of roasting meat filled the air.

The fight ring sat front and center in the outside area. Rectangular, surrounded by ropes, it looked like a small boxing ring.

Vander scanned around. He couldn't see a certain annoying brunette.

"Beer?" A stacked woman in a strapless, red dress and a mass of black curls stopped in front of him. Her lips were painted the same color as her dress. She held up two bottles of Bud and licked her lips.

"No, thanks," he said.

She cocked her head. "Anything else I can tempt you with?"

"Not right now."

"Go, Charlene." Trucker appeared.

The woman pouted and sidled away.

"Figured you'd turn up for a change." Trucker sipped his beer. "Your hot little mechanic is fitting right in." Trucker tilted his head.

Vander's muscles tightened as he followed the biker's gaze.

Fuck.

Brynn was sitting on a table, her long legs crossed. She was wearing a tiny denim skirt and a black halter top that molded to her torso. Her hair was out.

She had so much hair. All those fascinating strands of brown, gold, tan, and caramel.

Several bikers crowded around her. She laughed and sipped her drink. They watched her like she was a juicy steak, and they were vicious guard dogs, pulling at their chains.

Grill, Trucker's second in command, leaned in and toyed with her earring. The guy was about Vander's age and height, and all muscle. He kept his brown hair shaved short, had a moustache, and a tattoo of a snake circling his neck. He looked besotted, but Vander knew the guy had a violent temper and liked to cut people.

Vander didn't want the asshole anywhere near Brynn. What the hell was she thinking, smiling and flirting with these guys? She'd done her homework, so she was too smart not to know that she was playing with fire. She had to know what Grill was like.

Vander managed to keep from showing any of that on his face. "She gets hurt, Trucker, you'll answer to me."

The biker's eyes narrowed. "I'm not a babysitter, Norcross. You said she can handle herself."

"You'll answer to me," Vander repeated.

"Always fucking lording it over everyone. Getting into Wanderers business."

Vander turned, his gaze solely on Trucker. "You got a problem, Trucker?"

The man's body jerked. "No, no problem."

Vander looked back at Brynn. "Good. You got some new blood?"

"Yeah." The biker took another swig of beer.

"Where from?" Vander asked.

"All around." Trucker looked away.

Vander noted some of the new faces. Couple of big guys in leather. One with lots of ink, and the other with a huge, bushy beard. Another, slimmer, man with a wide smile for the woman clinging to him.

Vander would get Ace to run some searches on them all. One of them was the new drug supplier, and from Trucker's face, he was scared.

Grill slung an arm around Brynn. She looked like she was trying to slide out from under it. When the biker pressed a hand to her thigh, Vander ground his teeth together, and strode toward them. The crowd parted for him.

Brynn's head shot up and locked on him.

Grill was oblivious, sliding his hand up dangerously close to the hem of her skirt.

Vander grabbed the back of Grill's vest and yanked him backward.

The man staggered and spun. "What the fuck!" He saw Vander and went still, like a snake had just popped out of the grass.

"Bry," Vander said.

"It was nothing, V. Just having a good time." She slid off the table.

Vander grabbed her, hauling her to his side. "Let's get a drink."

Grill just glared silently. With an arm around her, Vander headed toward the bar. She slid her arm around his waist, but he noted that she was as stiff as a board.

"Norcross—"

He spun her into him. He was shocked to find that

she fit him perfectly. Just the perfect height to mold against his body.

He slid a hand into her hair and tilted her head back. He saw the pulse hammering in her throat, and stroked his thumb along her jaw.

Her chest hitched, but he was mesmerized by those damn freckles sprinkled across her nose.

"Grill is dangerous," he said.

She made an annoyed sound. "Everyone here is."

"You need to tread lightly."

She went up on her toes, their faces inches apart. "Norcross, the most dangerous man here is you."

"Not to you."

"Bullshit," she muttered.

He stared at her lips. Fuck, he wanted to taste them. Would she be tart and bite him? Or would she go soft and taste sweet?

He rubbed his thumb over her lips.

She shuddered. "What are you doing?"

What the hell was he doing? He released her. "Let's get those drinks."

She blinked, like she suddenly remembered where they were, and looked around. People watched with varying degrees of curiosity, jealousy, and interest. Some were whispering.

Vander saw Grill staring at them. He stared back, and let his hand slide around Brynn's denim-encased hip. Grill's glare intensified, then his face twisted and he looked away.

Brynn grabbed Vander's shirt. "I know what you're doing," she whispered furiously.

He cocked a brow.

"Branding me the property of Vander Norcross."

"If it helps keep you safe…"

"It means people won't open up to me," she whispered.

"That's your problem, not mine."

"You were just supposed to do the introduction, not tell everyone I'm yours."

He gripped her chin. "If they think you're mine, it might keep you alive."

"Argh, I really want to punch you."

He really wanted to kiss her. Damn, that face. Those angry eyes. Vander's body responded, cock hardening at the thought of tangling with the detective while she was angry.

"Save it for later." He dredged up some control. "Let's get a drink, then take a look at the new Iron Wanderers members. See if we can narrow down this new dealer."

Her nose wrinkled. "Fine."

CHAPTER FOUR

B rynn took the drink Vander handed her, and tried to wrangle her anger into some sort of submission.

She was a woman in a male-dominated profession, and she was very used to knocking overprotective, patronizing men out of her way.

She was well-aware Vander Norcross wouldn't be so easy.

And she'd just been branded his... Girlfriend sounded too lame. Norcross wouldn't have a girlfriend. Woman.

Vander Norcross' woman.

Tension curled low in her belly. She sipped her drink. It was soda water masquerading as vodka.

"You going to ignore me?" he asked.

"No. How did you explain my alcohol-free drink to the bartender?" Everyone around them was well on their way to getting plastered.

"I told him I liked my woman sober when I fucked her."

Brynn choked on her drink and met his dark gaze.

She couldn't tell much from that blank face, but she was pretty sure he was amused.

She arched a brow. "Do you?"

The corner of his lips quirked. "Want to find out?"

Yes. *No.* She tried to find some control over her hormones. "No. I want to find an asshole dealer." She studiously looked away from him and at the crowd. "The new guys are over there by the fight ring with Grill."

Vander turned. He held a bottle of beer, but she noted that he hadn't drunk any of it.

No, a man like Vander Norcross probably rarely let his guard down enough to get drunk.

"The big guy with the beard is Robert 'Shotgun' Rice," she said. "Was an enforcer for a club in Chicago. The tall one with the ink is 'Bender' Winslow. I didn't catch his first name. The small guy with the charm is Tony 'Nomad' Garcia. He's from Arizona, and seems to be a bit of a player." As they watched, Nomad kissed the woman beside him with lots of tongue.

Classy.

"You get a gut feel from any of them?" Vander asked.

"Nothing yet." She saw Grill look her way, then shoot an angry glare at Vander. "You made an enemy of Grill."

Vander just raised a brow, looking so outrageously hot and unconcerned. He was wearing all black tonight. He'd ditched the suit for black jeans and a tight, black Henley with the sleeves pushed up. His leather jacket was black as well. It just added to his dangerous aura.

Shouts and cheers rose from around the fight ring. Two big bikers were inside, really beating each other up.

Vander moved in behind her. They shifted closer to the ring.

An edgy energy pumped off the crowd. Blood lust was building. She felt it vibrate through her.

Grill leaped up on the ropes, roaring at the fighters and egging them on.

When she glanced up, Vander wasn't watching the fight. He was watching the new club members. That midnight gaze didn't miss much. Brynn wondered if he ever switched off. Did he relax? Did he ever stop being lethal, scary Vander Norcross and just be a man?

What would it take to gain his trust? To get under that sexy, bronze skin of his?

She whipped her head back to the fight, her heart thumping. Those were dangerous, dangerous thoughts.

With a giant left cross, one of the fighters took the other down. His opponent fell like a giant redwood, back slamming into the floor.

The crowd went wild.

Brynn wasn't sure she'd learn much else tonight. Her informant, a woman called Tonya who was the old lady of a low-level Wanderer member, was here, but Brynn didn't want to risk talking with her. Brynn had helped Tonya and her kid out of an abusive relationship. She was a nice lady, but apparently, she had a radar for dangerous men.

Brynn barely held back a snort. Ironic when she had the most dangerous man in San Francisco pressed up against her back.

"Who's next?" the winning fighter roared from the center of the ring.

Grill leaped over the ropes and the crowd cheered. The biker turned and pointed at Vander.

Brynn went rigid. *Oh, no.*

Vander just looked calmly at Grill. Like the man was inviting him to share a beer.

"You a pussy, Norcross?" Grill roared. "All bark and no bite."

The crowd hollered.

Brynn turned. "Just ignore him."

A faint smile tipped Vander's lips. "You trying to protect me?"

"Vander, these guys pound on each other for fun. You don't have to do this." She pressed her hands to his chest. He was so damn hard.

"I can handle Grill."

"Vander—"

He leaned down and ran his nose along the side of hers. It was an intimate, unexpected move, and heat pooled low in her belly.

Then he shrugged off his jacket and handed it to her.

Her stomach cramped. *No.*

Then he pushed up his sleeves, and she was caught by his sexy, muscled forearms. Other, more heated, things filled her belly now.

"I'll be back."

Sucking in a breath, she spun and watched him leap up, then climb into the fight ring.

Grill was in the center, bouncing on his feet. Eagerness wafted off the biker. There was an ugly smile on his face.

He threw a few test punches into the air.

Both men were about the same height. Brynn's lungs were tight as she looked them over. Vander looked cool, almost bored. Grill was pumping himself up.

God, this was not going to end well. She hid her nerves. What was Vander thinking?

She moved closer to the fight ring, jostled by the crowd around her.

Vander had military training. Not just any training, but the best. She knew he could wipe the floor with Grill. But the biker was riled and mean, and wouldn't fight fair.

The crowd sensed the hot tension, and the shouting and cheering increased in volume.

"Gonna mess you up, Norcross!" Grill pulled off his vest and T-shirt. Slabs of muscle covered his chest and his skin was covered in ink.

There was no reaction from Vander.

Grill hopped from one foot to the other. "I'm going to show everyone that you aren't so tough."

"You going to talk me to death?" Vander drawled.

Anger rippled over the biker's features. He charged, arm swinging.

But Vander wasn't there.

He sidestepped with a lethal grace that made Brynn gasp.

Grill turned and swung again.

Vander dodged.

Every time Grill attacked, Vander evaded. It was like he could predict Grill's moves before he made them.

"I'm not messed up yet," Vander said dryly.

Fury ignited on Grill's face. He was working himself up. With a roar, he charged.

Vander moved fast. He sidestepped, gripped the back of Grill's neck, and gave him a shove.

The biker ran headfirst into the ropes.

Some people in the crowd gasped. A few laughed.

Damn. Vander was just humiliating the guy.

Grill spun, his nostrils flaring, his breathing hard.

"You done?" Vander asked.

"Fight me!"

"You sure that's what you want?"

"I'm going to kill you," Grill barked.

Vander's smile was a cold thing. "Sure."

Suddenly, Grill yanked a knife out of his boot.

The crowd gasped. Weapons were against the rules, and Brynn's pulse spiked.

Grill brandished it and charged.

And Vander was clearly done.

He landed a hard chop to the biker's arm and blocked the slice of the knife. Then he launched a vicious jab to Grill's face.

His head snapped back, and the crowd went silent. The biker looked dazed, and shook his head.

Brynn wasn't a fan of unnecessary violence, so she was shocked to find she was outrageously turned on. Vander's calm, ruthless attitude had her panties soaked.

She glanced around and saw other women were watching him with hungry awe.

Another hard, unforgiving punch, and Grill dropped facedown to the floor of the fight ring.

And didn't move.

He hadn't landed one hit on Vander.

Vander coolly scanned the now-silent crowd. Nearby,

Trucker looked at Grill and shook his head.

Then the crowd burst into whistles and applause.

Vander's midnight gaze met Brynn's.

She felt like the air was sucked away. An arc of something hot shot between them, and her skin heated.

Then Vander climbed out of the fight ring and stalked toward her.

VANDER'S BLOOD PUMPED THICKLY. As he strode through the crowd, he was aware of everyone, but his focus narrowed to one person.

Her.

All he could see was Brynn. She watched him, and lifted her chin. There was that spark in her eyes. The one that said she saw him, and could meet him toe to toe.

Right in that moment, for the first time in a very long time, Vander didn't weigh the odds, calculate the risk, or consider the consequences.

He didn't care who or what she was, or who she was related to.

He reached her, snaked an arm around her and yanked her against him.

She didn't push him away or say anything. No, she did the opposite of what he expected.

She wrapped herself around him.

Fuck. Desire was a hot lick of flame in his gut. Her breasts pressed against his chest, and Vander felt something inside of him snap.

He lifted her off her feet, lowered his head, and

closed his mouth over hers.

The dark taste of her hit him. A hand slid into his hair as he sank into the kiss.

Her clever tongue stroked his and with a growl, he deepened the kiss. He pulled her closer, her breasts rubbing against his chest. The kiss ignited something in him, setting him on fire. It licked his skin, sank into his bones.

She moaned into his mouth, and the kiss went wild— with tongue, lips, and teeth.

It was the hooting and hollering of the crowd that brought him to his senses.

Vander lifted his head.

Fuck. They were in the middle of a wild, crowded biker party.

Brynn's blue eyes met his, sparkling like crystal. Her lips parted, and her breathing was coming in pants. She didn't look away.

He set her down.

"Norcross." Trucker slapped his shoulder. "I'd keep one eye open for Grill. He'll be gunning for you after that."

There were two new fighters in the ring now. Grill had apparently come to, and slunk off to lick his wounds.

Trucker grinned. "Get your woman out of here. You two look like you have better ways to celebrate."

Vander just lifted his chin and took Brynn's hand.

He led her out of the party, ignoring some very obvious invitations from a few biker babes. He felt Brynn's fingers flex in his, and then they were out on the street.

"So, Grill really isn't your fan," she said.

"I'm heartbroken," Vander said. "You got your bike?"

"No, I got an Uber."

Keeping hold of her, he started toward his X6. He could still taste her on his lips. He flexed his free hand. "I'll drop you home."

"Are we going to talk about that kiss?"

Shit. Of course, Brynn would wade straight in and not dance around it. He kept silent.

"Was it just to make it clear to those people in there that I'm the property of Vander Norcross?"

It would be so easy for him to say yes. Let her believe it was all just part of her cover.

"No. It was a mistake." He stopped by the X6 and turned to face her. She was partly in shadow.

"It was. A *big* mistake." She tossed her mass of brown hair over her shoulder. "It's done now. We move on and do our jobs."

Vander cocked his head. Her tone was all no-nonsense. It irritated him that she could shrug it off, like swatting an annoying fly.

He stepped forward, pinning her against the SUV.

"Hey." She pressed a hand to his chest. "You just said the kiss was a mistake."

"I know." He pressed an arm to the vehicle above her head.

She smelled like fresh soap—no cloying perfumes or creams for the detective.

"So back up," she said.

"No." He leaned in, their breaths mingling. "Why haven't you punched me yet, Detective?"

"I'm thinking about it."

"Really?"

"Damn you, Norcross." With her eyes on his, she cupped his face and pulled his mouth to hers.

Fuck. Again, she was a jolt to his system, and he wasn't sure he liked it.

He pressed against the cool metal and ravished her mouth. She bit his lip, and he ran his hands down that fit, compact body.

Desire exploded, urging him to take her. Take what he needed.

The ringing of a cell phone broke the moment.

She broke the kiss and cursed, fumbling in her pocket. "Goddammit." She yanked out the phone. "Sullivan."

He watched her face change. It hardened, a tough look entering her eyes. She cursed, instantly looking every inch a cop.

"Where? Okay, I'll be there as soon as I can."

"What happened?" he demanded.

She slid the phone away, and set her hands on her hips. She sucked in a breath. "Drugs turned up at a dance party in SoMa."

He heard the cutting anger in her voice. "And?"

"Stardust. And now a kid is dead. I need a ride to headquarters, then—"

"Give me the address. I'll take you."

"Vander, that's—"

"It would be faster if you don't argue."

Her lips flattened. "Fine."

He circled the SUV while she climbed into the

passenger seat. She told him the address in the South of Market area, not too far from his place. He started the engine.

"My colleagues are interviewing everyone at the party. The dealer was there earlier, selling his goods. He said it was high-quality. Asshole." She slammed a palm on the dash.

Vander wondered what poor teenager had made a bad and fatal choice. "You can't save them all, Detective."

She sat back in her seat, massaged her temple. She looked tired and pissed. "I know. My father taught me that. Pick your battles, focus on who you can help."

"He's a cop?"

"Was. Died in the line of duty."

Pride, love, and grief. Vander heard them all. And damn, he found her an attractive combination—soft and firm, giving and tough. "I'm sorry."

"Thanks, it was a long time ago." She cleared her throat. "All the new Wanderers were here at the club-house tonight, but any one of them could've been at this dance party beforehand."

"Yes." It didn't help narrow it down. Fifteen minutes later, he pulled up at the warehouse. There was a string of police cars and ambulances out front. He noted the crowd huddled behind the police tape.

Brynn was out of the SUV before he'd turned off the engine. He followed her, and watched her brisk strides as she slipped under the tape with a nod to a uniform.

An older detective ambled over. His shirt was rumpled, his hair equally disheveled. It took Vander a second to place him. Detective Mike Jankowski. Twice divorced, but a solid cop.

"Nice outfit, Sullivan." Jankowski eyed her bare legs and cowboy boots.

It was an attempt to lighten the mood, but Vander could tell the situation was too grim for the teasing comment to do much.

"One dead?" she confirmed.

"Yeah. Three in the hospital getting their stomachs pumped. A few high, dizzy, and puking."

"What a mess." Her jaw worked, then she stiffened.

He followed her gaze. The paramedics were pushing a gurney out of the warehouse, with a body covered by a sheet on it.

"Sarah Bello. Age twenty-one," Jankowski said.

"Fuck." Brynn rested her hands on her hips.

"Nothing you can do for her," Vander said.

He'd long ago gone numb to dead bodies. In Ghost Ops, he'd seen too many die, in far too many different ways. Some friends, fellow soldiers, allies, and enemies. Too many women and children.

Brynn looked up at him, and there was something stark in her eyes. "I can find the person responsible. I can stand up for her and stop the asshole."

She pivoted and strode toward the witnesses, who were still wearing their party clothes but huddled under blankets. One was retching into a bucket.

Vander watched Brynn and thought of that look in her eyes.

She was a woman who understood the darkness he'd seen. A woman who danced with it, as well.

CHAPTER FIVE

W hat a damn waste.

Brynn was tired to the bone as she left the crime scene. The victim's body was long gone, and she thought of the devastated family.

Her stomach cramped. That poor girl. Her poor loved ones.

Brynn rubbed her temple. She'd worked all day, then gone to the Wanderers party, and now she'd seen a young woman's life extinguished forever.

Anger was a low simmer in her veins, but she was too tired to deal with it tonight. She needed to get home and crash. She'd find an officer to give her a lift.

She ducked under the tape and saw Vander leaning against his sleek SUV.

She felt a funny sensation in her chest. She realized she always would. Vander Norcross would always pack a punch, no matter how many times she saw him.

"You didn't have to hang around."

He had his ankles crossed and his hands in the pockets of his jeans. "I'll drop you home."

Too tired to argue, she just nodded.

"How are the kids at the hospital?"

"Looks like they'll make it."

He brushed past her as he opened the door of the SUV. He still smelled of his ocean cologne, mixed with his male scent. It was a nice change from the stench of vomit.

"You all right?" he asked.

"No. Seeing a young person, who had their life ahead of them, cut short..." Anger swelled and she shook her head. "It gets to me. Sarah will never graduate college, or fall in love, or walk down the aisle on her father's arm, or have children."

"You told me you can't save them all."

"No, I can't, but I know her now. Her face. Her lost dreams. So, I'll mourn her and get her justice."

He shifted closer, and she pressed a hand to his chest. Her brain was foggy from the tiredness.

"I don't have the energy to deal with you right now, Norcross."

"I know." He tucked her hair behind her ear. "Guess you'll just have to let me look after you and get you home."

"Fine. But no funny business." She climbed in.

"Funny business?"

"Yes, with your clever mouth, and sexy, hard body."

He gave her a slow smile. "You think I'm clever and sexy?"

Oh, shit. She needed to stop talking. She looked straight ahead, out the windshield. "I'm really tired. You can't trust what I say right now. But I'm pretty certain you know what you look like, and how good you can kiss."

He made an amused sound.

Brynn closed her eyes. "I'm going to stop talking now."

He circled the vehicle and climbed into the driver's seat. He smoothly pulled out onto the street.

She opened up one eye to watch him. He had strong hands, and he drove in that easy, competent way that was so sexy.

She realized those hands had taken lives, and protected lives. They were hands that she really, really wanted to feel on her skin.

Shit. She really needed some sleep.

The next thing she knew, hands were touching her. She jerked, forming a fist.

"Easy there, Detective. Time to wake up. We're at your place."

"I wasn't asleep." She looked into Vander's face. He was leaning over the center console and unclipping her belt.

A flash of amusement crossed his cool face. "Right. You were just thinking with your eyes closed."

"Yes." She slid out. They were in front of her apartment building. She was so foggy-headed, and she just wanted to collapse in her bed.

Vander met her on the sidewalk.

"Thanks for the ride," she said.

He nodded.

She forced her feet to move toward the lobby door.

"Brynn, that girl's death is not your fault. You can't carry that guilt around."

She paused and looked back at him. She got the impression he was speaking from experience. "I know, but I will for a little while. It's hard to switch off, isn't it?"

"Yeah."

Something in his voice, and the look in his eye, sent a shiver through her. Everyone looked at Vander Norcross and saw strength and power. Did no one ever look past that? She walked back to him until only an inch separated them.

"It'll help when I stop the dealer and know that he can't hurt anyone else." She reached up and touched Vander's jaw.

He went motionless.

"You've stopped a lot of bad people, Vander. That means you've saved lives."

He stared at her, like he couldn't quite work her out. "It's easy to forget, and to just remember the bad stuff."

Brynn felt so drawn to him. Like he was a magnet and she was pure metal. She leaned closer...

"Brynn?" a male voice called out from the lobby doorway.

She glanced back and saw a familiar, tall, broad-shouldered frame that leaned toward lanky, silhouetted by the light.

"You okay?" the man asked.

"Fine," she said. "I'm coming in now."

"I'll make you some tea."

Vander stiffened and stepped back. "You live with someone?"

"Yes."

"A man."

Oh, that lethal tone was back. His face completely shut down.

"Yes, my brother."

Vander frowned and she fought back her amusement.

"Bard's a firefighter."

Vander studied her brother's shadow. "He looks ready to come out here and drag you in."

"Well, it is late, and I am loitering in the street with a dangerous man."

"You always have a quick comeback, don't you?"

She snorted. "I have three siblings. I learned fast."

"I have three siblings, too."

They both smiled, a shared moment of understanding.

Oh, no. She really shouldn't start to see Vander Norcross as a brother, a son, a man.

"Brynn, you coming?" Bard sounded ticked.

"In a minute," she snapped back.

She saw Vander's lips quirk, which made her gaze get stuck on them. He lifted a hand and played with her hair. Her breath hitched.

"You did well tonight," he said.

She widened her eyes. "High praise, coming from you."

"When Hunt first floated this idea, I was sure it was going to go south."

"I don't like to fail."

"I see that."

"And I'm a middle child. I always had to fight for what I wanted, or I'd miss out. I always get what I go after."

He tugged on her hair. "Be careful with Trucker and the Wanderers. And if you need help, call me."

"I don't have your number."

"I'll send it to you."

"You don't have my number," she said.

"My tech guy can have your number in thirty seconds."

"Or you could just ask Hunt. All normal, and legal-like."

A faint tilt of his lips. "But much less fun." He looked at her mouth for a second, and she thought he'd touch her again.

Then he stepped back. "Good luck, Detective."

He got back in his sexy SUV and drove off. Brynn watched the brake lights disappear around a corner, fighting back a strange sense of loss, then headed toward the door.

Her brother scowled at her. "Who the hell was that?"

"Someone helping me with my Wanderers case."

"I didn't get a good look at him in the dark, but he didn't look like a biker."

"He's not."

"Still, I got the impression he's not a man to mess with."

Wasn't *that* the truth. They walked inside, and Brynn's eyes burned. "I need my bed."

"Come on then, sis." He grimaced at her short skirt.

"Where the hell did you get that scrap of nothing? And don't let Mom see those fake tats."

Brynn rolled her eyes. "Can you save the disapproving brother routine for the morning?" She yawned.

"Yeah. Come on, sleeping beauty."

Her phone pinged as they waited for the elevator. She pulled it out and saw a message from an unknown number.

Be careful.

Damn, Vander was good.

She stepped into the elevator, and Bard tugged on her hair.

But it was thoughts of another man doing it that stuck in her head.

―――――

VANDER SAT at the head of the conference room table, his hands steepled under his chin.

Ace Oliveira had finished giving a debrief on a cyber security job he'd just completed. Vander was listening, but he was thinking about Brynn.

It had been three days since the Wanderers party. Three days since he'd dropped her home. Three days since he'd kissed her.

He hadn't heard a peep from her. He kept wondering if she was okay.

"Vander?"

He looked up at Saxon. His best friend was staring at him with a frown.

All the guys were watching him.

"Anything else?" Vander asked.

They all shook their heads.

"Good." Vander rose. "I'm hitting the gym." He didn't normally work out in the middle of the day, but he needed to work off some of this edginess. He needed to stop thinking about a certain police detective.

"Vander?" Saxon grabbed his arm. "Are you okay?"

"Yeah. I just need to burn off some energy."

"I'm pretty sure you need to get laid." Saxon grinned. "That's a particular upside of having a fiancée. Regular sex."

Vander growled. "I do not want to hear about you, sex, and my sister. Ever."

"You sure you're okay?"

Vander just waved a hand dismissively and stomped downstairs to the Norcross gym.

He pulled his workout gear out of the locker, changed, and then hit the treadmill.

He set the speed fast. For a little while, he thought of nothing but his breathing and the burn in his legs. After ten miles, he stepped off and grabbed a towel.

An image of Brynn in that tiny skirt popped into his head. Her smile. That twinkle in her eyes when she looked at him. Her freckles.

Shit. Growling, he headed for the weights and started some bicep curls.

She'd be fine. Hunt had said she was good, and the little time Vander had spent with the detective had shown him that she was competent.

But the Wanderers were rough. And this new guy muscling in meant there were dangerous tensions.

He set the weights down and dropped down on the mat to do some crunches.

He hit a hundred and kept going.

"Man, what is with you today?"

Vander turned his head to see his brother, Rhys, lounging in the doorway.

"Nothing."

His brother rolled his eyes. "I know you like to be a fortress of solitude, bro, but you don't need to be the stoic commander all the time. Not anymore."

Vander sat up. "I have some things on my mind." He shook his head. "I'll sort it out."

And get the off-limits detective out of his thoughts.

"Haven's planning a dinner party with the gang. She wants you to bring a date."

"No."

"Vander, you know I do everything in my power to make my woman happy."

"I bring a woman to a family thing, they get ideas I don't want them having."

Rhys shoved a hand through his hair. "Wouldn't hurt you to find a woman. You find the right one, and she makes everything better."

Vander grunted and pushed to his feet. Since his brothers and sister had all happily hooked up with the loves of their lives, they couldn't help but matchmake.

"It's finding the right one that makes the difference, right?" An image of a face dotted with freckles hit him. *Fuck.* "You seemed to enjoy variety until then."

"True," Rhys agreed.

"Tell Haven I'll think about it, but not to count on it."

"Roger that."

Ace appeared, tablet in hand, and a frown on his face. "Vander, you know why an informant named Twitch is trying to reach you?"

Vander straightened. Twitch was a member of the Blades. The street gang wasn't huge, and they usually tried to steer clear of the larger, more dangerous Norteños or MS-13. Twitch usually had good intel.

"No. I'll call him."

After a quick shower and a change back into his suit, Vander headed up to his office. He scrolled through his contacts to find Twitch, and called.

There was no answer.

Shrugging, Vander sat and got busy with some work. He didn't love being stuck in the office, but paperwork was a necessary evil to running a business.

Every now and then, he found himself staring out the window, wondering what Brynn was doing. Were the asshole Wanderers giving her a hard time? He gritted his teeth. None of this was his damn business.

What about Grill? Vander wasn't dumb enough to just dismiss him. The asshole wasn't the type to back off.

Vander's fingers itched to dial Hunt and ask for an update.

Shit. Rhys was right, he really needed to get laid.

He focused back on his paperwork. And lasted ten minutes.

Fuck it. He grabbed his phone and found her number.

Everything good?

He had no idea where she was, or if she would even respond.

His phone vibrated.

Everything's good.

That was it? He tapped his screen.
How's the new job?

Busy and not quite as enlightening as I'd hoped.

She hadn't uncovered the dealer yet.
Sorry to hear that.

You been busy skulking in the shadows?

There was that smart mouth.
I don't skulk.

You made me snort laugh. You are the very definition of a skulker.

Thieves and bad guys skulk. I move with stealth.

I don't know. I'm still not convinced.

Vander shook his head and found himself smiling.

Hey, did you catch the Sharks game last night? They smashed the Blues. Told you that they'd claw back.

I saw it. They got lucky. They play the Bruins next and they don't have a chance.

Bite your tongue. How about a little friendly wager? They win, you owe me a marker. I hear a favor from you is a valuable commodity.

What do I get when I win?

What do you want?

He stared at the words on the screen. Dangerous thoughts twisted through him.

I'll think of something. You're on.

You're going down. Now, I have to go.

Be careful.

I always am. Go Sharks!

He shook his head, still smiling. She was okay, that was all that mattered.

Then his phone rang. An unknown number. He pressed it to his ear. "Norcross."

"Hey, Vander." Nervous breathing.

"Heard you were looking for me, Twitch. What have you got?"

There was an audible swallow. "Blades are getting a big Stardust delivery. Huge."

Vander stiffened. "Really? From?"

"Bikers. The Iron Wanderers."

Vander's fingers curled into a fist.

"They have some new guy. He's making all kinds of promises."

"When's the delivery?" Vander asked.

"Shit. If my brothers find out I talked, I'm dead."

"I'm not planning to tell your gang leader."

More heavy breathing. "Security will be tight. There will be Blades and bikers."

"When?" Did Brynn know?

"Tonight. Midnight."

The heart of darkness. "Where?"

"Shit, Norcross. I'm not high enough up to have all the deets. Somewhere neutral. That's all I got."

"Okay, Twitch. You did well."

"I'll get my next payment?"

"Yeah."

"Thanks, Norcross." The call ended.

Vander rose and rapped his knuckles on the desk. He needed to find out where that delivery was happening. The new dealer was sure to be there. He definitely wasn't wasting any time making allies.

Now, did Vander inform Detective Sullivan?

He had no desire to see her wade into the middle of a dangerous drug drop.

And if she knew already...

Fuck. Vander needed to find out where the deal was going down.

He shrugged into his jacket and headed out of his office.

Saxon was out in the hall, holding a file. His best

friend raised a brow. "Where are you off to?"

"I need to visit some informants. Hold the fort?"

"Sure. Need a hand?"

"Not yet."

Vander strode down to the parking level to get his bike, telling himself this had nothing to do with Brynn Sullivan.

CHAPTER SIX

Brynn crept quietly through the darkness, careful not to make a sound. She was dressed all in black, blending in with the shadows.

If Hunt knew she was here alone, he'd be pissed.

But there was a good chance she'd finally nail down who the new dealer was.

The last few days, she'd spent a lot of time at the Iron Wanderers garage, supplying parts, and subtly pumping bikers for information.

Slowly, they were starting to trust her a little. Not Grill. He avoided her, and glared at her when they crossed paths. He had a killer black eye.

And just like that, she thought of Vander.

The hard, powerful body. The face. The cool, controlled façade. The way he'd destroyed Grill without breaking a sweat.

She fought back a shiver.

His text message today had been a surprise. She

shouldn't be thinking about him, let alone texting with him and making wagers on hockey games.

He'd also managed to star in her dreams, damn him. Last night, she'd finally given in and pulled out her vibrator.

And come hard, imagining Vander Norcross inside her.

Her womb clenched, and she cursed under her breath.

She was creeping around an empty warehouse facility in the middle of the night, so she needed to focus, not fantasize about the most dangerous man in San Francisco.

At the Wanderers, she'd overheard whispers about a drug deal with the Blades.

It burned her to let any drugs into the hands of gang members, but she had to stop this dealer. She couldn't screw this deal.

"I am going to stop you," she whispered.

The deal was happening at a delivery center. The large parking lot was empty at this time of night, except for a row of parked delivery trucks. The huge warehouse loomed above her.

From what she'd heard, the deal would go down soon. It was scheduled to happen at the southern end of the warehouse at midnight.

She'd parked blocks away and slipped in over the fence.

She eyed the building. The best bet for a good view, and not getting caught, would be the roof.

Brynn found a drainpipe and then tightened the straps of her small backpack. She gripped the pipe and climbed.

She was grunting and straining by the time she reached the top. Thank God she worked out frequently. She was always giving Jankowski a hard time for being unfit, and dragging him out for a run. She also ran with her brother, when their schedules meshed.

She pulled herself onto the roof and crouched. It was cloudy tonight, so there was no stray moonlight to spotlight her. Staying crouched, she walked across the large, pitched roof.

She crested the peak, and carefully climbed down the other side.

An engine rumbled, and she saw a flash of headlights.

Brynn ducked low and watched. A nondescript van pulled into the yard below.

Hello.

She silently crept closer to the edge, carefully slipping her backpack off her shoulders. Another vehicle followed the van.

A dark-colored truck. Ford F250. Four Harleys rumbled in line behind the truck.

Near the roof's edge, she lay flat and unzipped the backpack. She pulled out her binoculars and zoomed in.

The van was parked, with four men who were obviously Blades beside it. They moved to the back of the van.

As the truck and bikes pulled up, she scanned the faces, but the bikers didn't look familiar. *Damn.*

From this angle, the dark, tinted windows of the truck made it impossible to see who was inside.

"Come on," she muttered.

A Blade member wandered over to the truck. The passenger door opened on the far side.

Nervous energy filled her. They were talking, but she still couldn't see the dealer.

The bikers began to unload boxes from the back of the truck, and two Blades opened the back of the van.

Dammit, from this vantage, unless the dealer got out, she wasn't going to get a good look.

"Spot anything, Detective?"

The low murmur beside her made her jolt. Only her training kept her hands tight on the binoculars.

She whipped her head to the side. Vander was just a dark shadow settling in beside her.

Dammit to hell. She hadn't heard him or sensed him at all. Damn, he was good.

"What are you doing here?" she whispered.

"Heard a deal was going down tonight. Have you seen the dealer?"

She released a breath and looked back at the transaction taking place below. "He's staying in the truck. I can't see him."

"Shit."

"You shouldn't be here." She lifted the binoculars. Still no dealer. She handed them to him.

He took them and looked through. "You can't hog all of the action, Detective."

"This is *my* case. I don't need you butting in."

He kept looking through the binoculars. "I like to keep my finger on the pulse of everything going down in my city."

"You mean you're a control freak."

"Brynn—" he lowered the binoculars "—it's much better to stay in control of things than to get blindsided when you least expect it."

The darkness was back. She heard it in his voice, and if it wasn't nighttime, she'd no doubt see it in his eyes. It lurked in him, and he obviously did his damnedest to control it.

"Hey, stay here with me," she said.

He gave the tiniest jerk. "I'm right here."

"You can't control everything, Vander."

He stiffened. "I can try."

"You can't just do what you want, when you want to. This is my investigation—"

"I'm not trying to take over."

"You should have called me and told me about the drop," she whisper-yelled.

She could feel him looking at her through the darkness.

"How come you're here alone, Detective? Shouldn't you have back up?"

She sniffed. "This is just surveillance."

"I think you don't mind bending the rules when it suits you," he said.

"At least I don't skirt right along the rules like they aren't even there," she hissed. "You do that long enough, you tip right over the edge, Norcross."

"Brynn—"

"I told you my father was killed in the line of duty. He got killed because his partner started taking bribes."

Vander was silent. "You're comparing me to a dirty cop."

She sighed. "No, dammit." She knew he wasn't anything like the man who'd betrayed her father.

"I do everything I can to help, not for my own selfish reasons." His voice was like a blade. "Life is messy, Brynn. It isn't neat and tidy, and it doesn't always follow the rules. We need the law, and we need people like you to uphold it. But sometimes, you need people like me who can sidestep things for the right reasons."

She stared at his dark shadow, her heart beating hard. She didn't entirely disagree with him, and the more she got to know him, the more she believed he lived and operated by his own private code.

One that would never see him take a bribe or hurt an innocent.

"*Fuck*," he bit out.

Brynn looked up and spotted another set of headlights approaching.

She snatched back the binoculars and zoomed in.

"Crap. The security company." She saw the logo on the side of the white sedan.

"Some rent-a-cop with a hero complex," Vander said. "He should've called it in."

Vander rose into a crouch.

Down below, the bikers and gang members scrambled.

She watched the familiar motions of pulling weapons.

No, no.

The security car stopped, and the doors opened.

"This is private property." Someone spoke through a megaphone. "You're trespassing. The police are on the way."

Brynn groaned.

There was a deep *woof*. A German Shepherd darted out of the security car and bounded towards the bikers and Blades.

Shit. She ground her teeth together.

Gunfire broke out.

Shit, shit, shit. The two security guards ducked down behind their vehicle. The bikers and gang members kept firing.

The dog leaped and hit one of the bikers, taking the screaming man down.

"This is a clusterfuck," Vander said. "We should go."

"We can't leave those guards." The gang members were advancing on the vehicle. "They're sitting ducks."

"You want to break your cover?"

She gritted her teeth. *Shit.* She knew the greater good was at stake, but she couldn't leave these men to die.

"Go," Vander said.

"Dammit, I can't—"

Vander lifted a Glock. "Get moving, Brynn." He aimed and fired.

A biker jerked and cried out.

Then Vander fired again and again. Pandemonium

exploded below. Bikers and Blade members dove for cover.

Brynn leaped up and ran along the roof.

She glanced back and watched the security car screeching in reverse, the dog running after it. Vander sprinted up the roof behind her, moving like a big, dark shadow.

Together, they scrambled down the other side.

"This way." He grabbed her hand and she felt that he was wearing gloves.

He pulled her to a stop at the edge, and she saw a rope dangling off the side of the warehouse.

Then he grabbed the rope and held it to her.

After a deep breath, Brynn gripped it and lowered herself over the edge. She climbed down. She wasn't elegant, but it did the job. Finally, her boots hit the concrete.

She looked up. Vander slid down the rope with an athletic grace that made her breath catch.

He landed beside her.

The sounds of shouts echoed through the night. The Iron Wanderers and the Blades would be looking for them.

"Time to run, Detective."

She nodded.

They sprinted across the lot, running behind the trucks. Vander stayed beside her with an easy stride that she suspected he could keep up for hours. They reached the fence.

He pulled out a set of wire-cutters and snipped the wire.

"Off you go," he said.

"But what—?"

He gripped her arm and their gazes met.

"Get out of here. There's nothing more you can do. Get home."

She hesitated. He was right, dammit. "Vander?"

His fingers tightened on her arm.

"I don't think you're anything like that dirty cop." She nodded, then climbed through the hole in the fence.

When she looked back, she watched him melt into the darkness and disappear.

Brynn turned and jogged all the way back to her car.

She slid inside. He'd be fine. It was an absolute waste of energy to worry about Vander Norcross.

She reached for the ignition and her phone vibrated.

Safe?

She'd saved his number as Badass Number One.

She tapped the screen.

Yes. You?

Fine. Go home, Detective. Get some sleep.

I'm pissed I didn't identify the dealer.

You'll get him. I have no doubt.

She felt a flush in her cheeks.

Well, thanks for the unasked-for assistance.

I never ask permission, Detective.

No, he was a man who simply took what he wanted.

Yes, yes, you're a badass. We all know.

You're asking for trouble, Brynn.
She bit her lip. Did she want trouble?
And the more important question, could she keep away from him?

Good night, Vander.

Night, Brynn. Sleep well.

THE NEXT MORNING, Vander gunned his bike, zipping through traffic as he headed for the Bay Bridge.

His hands flexed on the handlebars.

He shouldn't be heading to the Iron Wanderers club-house and garage. He should be at his office. He had a hundred jobs waiting for him.

But he wanted to see Brynn.

Last night, he'd watched her shimmy up the drain-pipe and creep across the roof. She was good.

Lying beside her...

He'd liked it way too much.

He knew she didn't fully accept the way he operated, but he also knew she understood that sometimes it was necessary. It made sense now why she'd had such a knee-jerk reaction. Her father had died because someone he trusted had broken the law. And Brynn was trying to live up to her father's legacy. He admired that.

Vander frowned under his helmet. He should stay away. She was Hunt's cousin; a cop. They were both good reasons to steer clear.

But that hadn't stopped him stroking his cock this morning while thinking about her. Detective Brynn Sullivan naked, wet, and hungry. She'd be an active participant in bed. She wouldn't let him lead all the time. Wouldn't let him have absolute control.

His cock throbbed.

Shit. He shifted on the bike.

He was just checking on her. That was it. Check in, let Trucker, Grill, and the Wanderers see him. Make sure they remembered she had his protection.

That was it. This was mainly for Hunt's benefit.

Vander pulled up outside the garage, and kicked the kickstand down. It was a warm day, so he wasn't wearing a jacket. He took a second to roll up his shirt sleeves.

Rock music was pumping from somewhere in the garage.

Silently, he walked inside. He took a second to appreciate the cooler temperature in the shadowed building. A pulled-apart bike sat in the first bay.

He heard voices and walked to the next one.

"Babe, we'd have a good time," a deep voice said.

He saw Brynn with a tall biker with long, shaggy hair. The man wore loose jeans and a white T-shirt. Today, Brynn was in another pair of tiny damn shorts, topped with a tight, black tank. Her brown hair was piled up on her head in a messy bun. A red bandanna was tucked into the back pocket of her shorts.

"No doubt, dude," she drawled. "But you need to back up. I have work to do on your bike."

"I like these sexy legs of yours. I want them in the air while I fuck you."

Rage began a slow crawl through Vander's chest.

The biker moved suddenly, pinning Brynn to the bike. "I want to fuck you right here." He shoved one hand between her legs while the other roughly grabbed her breast.

"*Hey*." There was outrage on her face, but no fear.

Still, the asshole outweighed her by a hundred pounds. As she struggled, he kept her pinned, groping.

"Women love my cock, babe. You'll like it."

"I said no, asshole. Let me go, and then I won't brain you with a wrench."

"I love when chicks play hard to get."

"I warned you." She swung a wrench up, catching his arm.

With a yelp, the biker stepped back.

"Bitch." He slapped her, the sound echoing in the space. "No one says no to me."

A red haze filled Vander's vision. He strode across the space.

Brynn saw him, and her eyes widened. "Vander—"

He dragged the guy off her. There was blood at the corner of her mouth.

Vander rammed his fist into the biker's gut. He methodically punched the man, over and over—gut, jaw, solar plexus. The man roared, and tried to hit back.

"You like attacking women?" Vander asked icily.

He punched the biker again, and the guy went down on one knee.

"Come on," Vander taunted. "It's easy to hit a woman smaller than you, but not so easy when you're facing me."

The biker heaved himself up and swung clumsily.

Vander punched the guy in the side and felt ribs crack. The man groaned.

"Vander, I'm okay," Brynn said.

Her voice was steady, calm. Of course, getting groped and hit by a giant biker wouldn't faze Detective Brynn Sullivan.

He met her gaze. She looked composed, cautious.

She held out a hand. "Vander—"

He looked away and landed another brutal punch to her attacker's face. The biker fell backward and landed heavily on the dirty floor.

"If I hear that you've attacked or touched any woman when she said no, I'll find you. And this will seem like fun." Vander grabbed Brynn's hand and pulled her outside.

"Vander—"

He didn't respond, barely processing her voice. He gripped her waist and lifted her to sit sideways on his bike.

She released a shaky breath. "The look on your face is downright scary. You look like you want to keep pummeling that guy."

"Don't tempt me." He gripped her jaw with a gentle hand, then wiped the blood away. She sucked in a breath, and he stroked her cheekbone.

"It's fine," she said quietly. "It doesn't feel too bad. I've been clocked before. This seems fine."

A muscle ticked in his jaw. He couldn't stop himself from brushing his fingers over her skin. Her chest hitched.

"He wanted to hurt you worse than this."

"And I would've stopped him." She reached up and gripped Vander's wrist. "I'm okay."

His fingers tightened on her. "I've seen men do horrible things. Overseas. The torture. The rape houses." His muscles clenched tight. "And it's not just over there. Bad stuff happens here, as well. I know it. I've seen it firsthand."

Her hands tightened on his wrist. "Vander, come back to me."

"Vowed to make sure my mother, my sister, my friends... None of them would ever be at risk. Promised to keep them safe."

"Oh, Vander. I'm okay." She slid off the bike and kissed him.

He was swamped by emotion. He fought every day to keep his emotions in check. When he felt too much, there wasn't anything he wouldn't do to protect those he cared about.

But even with that on his mind, he sank into the kiss, pulling her closer.

This woman...

She was dangerous to him.

A risk a man like him couldn't afford to take.

He pulled back, and liked that her breathing was as fast and unsteady as his.

"Vander…"

The tender way she said his name made his spine stiffen. "I think about you all the time."

She jolted, something flashing in those light-blue, crystal eyes. "I think about you, too."

"I don't want to. And I won't get entangled with you. I don't want your tangles, complications, or consequences."

Hurt flared before she hid it. "I thought you were a man who didn't worry about consequences."

"No, I'm the opposite. I've been well-trained by our government to assess the risk and eliminate the consequences."

"You're attracted to me," she whispered. "You want me."

He stayed silent.

"And I want you."

Fuck. His hands clenched on her. He couldn't risk her. What she could unleash in him…

He liked his world just as it was, but Brynn Sullivan would tear it wide open. She'd demand things, would stir things that were best left hidden.

"No. We're not doing this."

Her eyes sparked. "I never took you for a coward."

So many competing urges rose inside of Vander, threatening to swamp him.

"Norcross?" Trucker's gruff voice.

Vander stepped back and glanced over his shoulder. He spotted the biker on the sidewalk.

"Trucker, if that asshole in there touches her again, I'll kill him."

Trucker crossed his tattooed arms. "He's still groaning on the floor. Pretty sure he'll think twice before he breathes Bry's air again. We'll take care of it."

"Good."

Brynn glared up at Vander, then strode past him, purposely brushing his body with hers. She disappeared into the garage.

It took all of his self-control to pull his helmet on, climb on his bike, and ride away.

CHAPTER SEVEN

Getting ready for work the next morning, Brynn muttered angrily to herself and slammed a mug down on the kitchen counter.

Damn Vander Norcross.

He'd blown into her life, made her want him more than she'd ever wanted anyone, and then held himself back.

"*Men.*" She poured herself some coffee and scowled. How dare he kiss her? The best, sexiest, hungriest kisses she'd ever had, and then, he'd backed off? And to say that he didn't want her tangles and complications.

Fuck that. Being tangled up with her would be awesome.

"You keep staring at that coffee like that and it might explode." Her brother walked in, looking sleepy, wearing gray sweats and no shirt.

"I hate all men today, so watch out."

Bard held up his hands. "Hey, I didn't do anything."

"You have a Y chromosome." Brynn sipped her coffee, burned her tongue, and cursed.

Her brother touched her hair. "What's wrong, Bee?"

At the use of her childhood nickname, she blew out a breath. "There's a guy."

"Is it Jack?"

She frowned. "Who's Jack?"

"Nay's nice teacher guy from work."

"God, no."

"Want me to beat your guy up?"

"You wouldn't be able to," she said sourly.

"You usually do your own beating up. Even when you were little."

"He's interested, but he's holding back. He doesn't want to get 'involved.'" She waggled her fingers in air quotes. "He thinks I'm all trouble and complications."

Bard's lips quirked.

She pointed a finger at him. "Don't you dare take his side."

"You aren't simple, Brynn, not by a long shot." He tugged her hair. "And that's a good thing." He paused. "This the guy from the other night?"

"Yes." Thank God Bard hadn't seen who it was.

"What's his name? Is he a cop?"

"He's not a cop, and don't go all big brother on me."

"All right. So I take it Naomi's friend Jack doesn't have a chance?"

Brynn shot him a look.

Her brother grinned and poured his own coffee. As he sipped, he eyed her outfit. "I see you're still rocking the biker chick look today."

She was wearing sprayed-on jeans, and a tight, white tank with the Harley Davidson logo on it. "Yeah. I need to drop some parts off. I'm going to pop into headquarters first, and touch base with Hunt."

Bard frowned. "Be careful, Brynn."

"I will." She kissed his cheek. "You, too."

"And Bee, if that guy is smart, he'll come around. He won't be able to stay away."

An ache ignited in her belly. Bard didn't know Vander Norcross' iron will.

Brynn jumped on her Triumph and rode around for a while, until she was sure no one was following her, before heading into headquarters.

Her phone vibrated as she headed up in the elevator. It was a message from Carrin.

Heads up. Naomi is going to have another go at you about Jack.

Ugh. Brynn tapped into her phone.

Groan. I'm not interested.

Because of your new mystery guy.

Brynn sucked in a breath. God, her siblings were such nosy gossips.

OMG. Bard has a big mouth.

He's never seen you like this. Usually, you let guys slide right off you. Teflon is your middle name.

That's not true. I was totally in love with Brandon McGee.

Brynn, that's when you were twelve. It doesn't count.

This guy...it's new. And he's fighting it pretty hard.

Nothing worth having comes easily.
Brynn rolled her eyes.

Thank you, Teddy Roosevelt.

Oh, is that who said that?

Go prosecute a criminal.

Go catch one.

I would if my nosy siblings butted out of my love life.

Her sister signed off with a kiss emoji.

As Brynn strolled into the office area, she copped the teasing and wolf whistles around her outfit and tattoos. She headed for her office with a wave and an eye roll.

"Nice jeans, Sullivan!"

"Sullivan," Jankowski called out. "You can fix my engine any day."

"Your engine's too rusted, Jankowski," she yelled back.

Hoots of laughter followed.

"I hope my best detectives are behaving in a manner

becoming of the San Francisco Police Department," a deep voice said.

Lieutenant William Cook stepped into the room. Brynn's lips twitched. All the detectives suddenly looked very busy.

"Sullivan," the lieutenant said. "How's it going with the Wanderers?"

Lieutenant Cook was a tall man with a footballer's body. He had dark skin, black hair, and a jaw that would make a superhero proud. He was the kind of solid cop her father had been.

"Fine, sir. They seem to be accepting me so far. No ID on the new dealer yet."

"Okay, keep me posted. And keep your head down."

"Yes, sir."

Hunt appeared. The dark expression on his rugged face made her wince internally. He waved her into his office.

"Hey," she said.

He closed the door. "Word on the street is that Vander's branded you as his woman."

"Yes. He figured it would help explain why he'd recommended me to the club. And keep me safe. It was completely unnecessary."

Hunt crossed his arms over his chest. "That's all there is?"

"Yes." It wasn't exactly a lie.

"So, you weren't kissing him at a biker party?"

Brynn huffed out a breath. "It was part of the cover. Tobin 'Grill' Brady was hassling me."

Her cousin's frown deepened. "Grill is a psychopath."

"I can handle him. I didn't need Vander's heavy-handed, caveman tactics, but I'll work with it."

Hunt grunted. "Any progress?"

"Not as much as I'd like. I've had a few interactions with the new members, but nothing's popped. I like Shotgun, the former enforcer from Chicago, as the dealer. He's tough, experienced, and smart. Bender's from LA, and as far as I can tell, he's a biker to the core. He's all about riding and living free. Nomad from Arizona is a ladies' man. Flirts with me every time I see him, and from what I hear, he's already banged half the single biker babes in the club. He seems too laid-back and easy-going to be a drug-dealing mastermind."

"Whoever it is, he'll show his hand sooner or later."

She nodded. She was hoping for sooner. "I'm heading over to drop some parts at the garage. I have some for the new guys too. I might learn something."

"Okay. Brynn, steer clear of Vander."

She frowned. "You said you trusted him."

"With your safety, yes. With anything else, absolutely not."

Brynn grinned and patted her cousin's cheek. "You're cute when you go all big brother."

"Get out of here."

She headed to the impound lot when her phone pinged. It was a message from Naomi.

So, about Jack...

Ugh, her sister was like a dog with a bone.

NO.

At Impound, she collected the parts she needed from the ever-cheerful Manuel. The jovial officer was in his sixties, and had worked in impound for years. He was always happy.

"Here you go, Detective Sullivan. Everything you requested."

"Thanks, Manuel." She packed the parts into the saddlebags on her bike. "You and I could start a side business. We'd make a fortune selling parts."

He let out a loud, guffawing laugh. "Get out of here."

Brynn got on her bike. Her smile faded as she rode to Oakland. She pulled up at the Wanderers garage, and saw Trucker and two of the new guys—Bender and Nomad.

Trucker seemed a little edgier than usual. Was one of these guys the dealer? The one putting pressure on Trucker?

"Morning." She lugged in the parts.

"Hey, darlin'," Trucker said.

Bender nodded. Up close, she saw just how much ink he had.

Nomad smiled, all charm. "Hi, Bry."

"Here are the parts you wanted." She set them on the workbench.

"Fucking A." Nomad's smile widened. "Thanks."

She nodded. "I'll be next door, working on that Harley Low Rider."

She strolled through the doorway. Once in the neighboring bay, she tilted her head and listened to the murmur of the men's voices as they started talking.

The volume of the conversation dropped, and she crept closer to the doorway to listen.

"Fuck with me, Trucker, and you'll regret it." A low murmur.

Damn, she couldn't tell which of the bikers had spoken.

"Fuck you," Trucker growled.

"You and me will meet with Bones. He wants you there. A united front."

Trucker growled.

"The Back Corner Bar. We'll—"

She strained to hear what the men were saying. They were moving away, out of the bay.

"...three PM."

"Fuck you," Trucker spat again.

She peered around the doorway, and saw Trucker and the others stomping off.

Brynn tapped a finger on her lips. *The Back Corner Bar. Three o'clock.*

Her pulse tripped. This could be it. A meet between Trucker, the dealer, and some other player named Bones.

She made herself do some more work on the Harley, but her head was spinning. She needed to organize backup. She'd have to put an undercover officer in the bar.

Jankowski would do it.

She'd get there earlier, make it look like a coincidence that she happened to be there having a late lunch.

Excitement shot through her. *This was it.*

AT THREE O'CLOCK, she found herself playing pool with a big, African-American man called Billy. A half-eaten burger sat beside her, along with a half-empty beer. Her leather satchel rested close by with her SIG inside.

She was waiting for the guests of honor to arrive. She scanned the bar again, her gaze moving right through Jankowski, sitting at the bar, holding a beer.

He looked like he was brooding.

The door opened. The newcomer who strode in was too handsome for his own good. Jeans shaped muscular legs, and she was one-hundred-percent sure he'd have an excellent ass. His navy-blue T-shirt was so tight that the sleeves cut into his muscled biceps. Interesting tattoos flowed down his arms.

He headed for a table in the back, an eager waitress following him.

Wait. There was something about the way he moved...

Her gaze snapped back to his face and the dark, shaggy hair falling over his forehead.

Pieces clicked. *Rhys Norcross.*

Vander's younger brother, and top investigator.

Dammit to hell.

She took a few deep breaths, lined up her next shot, and took it.

"Hey, sugar," she said to Billy. "I need the ladies'. I'll be back soon."

Billy waved a finger at her. Brynn grabbed her bag and sauntered toward the ladies' room, and right by the table where the younger Norcross was sitting, tucked out of sight.

She paused. "Well, hello there." Anyone looking over would see her flirtatious smile and body language.

Only Rhys would see the angry glitter in her eyes.

He shot her a smile that made her breath catch. He was gorgeous, and he knew it. The strong jaw, and the thick hair that begged for a woman to run her hands through it. Yep, he had the Norcross good looks, through and through.

Funny, she wasn't anywhere near as attracted to him, as she was to the dark, lethal edge of his brother.

"What the hell would Rhys Norcross be doing here?" she asked, her voice dropping.

His smile widened. "You must be Brynn." His gaze dipped to her body, but to his credit, returned quickly to her face. "We heard a deal might be going down."

"And your brother asked you to drop by?"

"Maybe. Maybe I just wanted a burger."

"He asked you to keep an eye on me."

"Maybe." Rhys gave her another rock-star smile. "It's no hardship."

Brynn leaned closer, her seductive body language deceptive. "Tell your brother that I don't need a babysitter. And if you scare off the players, I'll slap you in cuffs so fast your head will spin."

His smile didn't dim. "Kinky."

She rolled her eyes. She straightened, shot him a saucy look, then sailed into the ladies' room.

When she came back out, she cruised by the bar.

"Bud," she told the bartender.

Jankowski swiveled on his stool. "Baby, where have you been all my life?" He eyed her chest with obvious interest.

A laugh welled up. She leaned in. "Cops always have the worst pickup lines." She snagged her fresh beer that she wasn't planning to drink, and sashayed away.

Back at the pool table with Billy, she sensed Rhys watching her. She was chalking her cue when Trucker walked in.

He spotted her and frowned.

"Bry, what are you doing here?"

"Hey, Trucker." She shot the cue a look, then nodded over at her pool partner. "I'm cleaning out Billy's pockets."

"She's good," Billy said.

"I like this place." She cocked her head. "You?"

"Having a beer. Meeting some people." He gave her a chin lift, then was gone.

As she played, she surreptitiously watched Trucker take a booth. He got an order of chicken wings and a beer.

Where was the dealer and this new contact?

Impatience rode her hard. *Come on. Come on.*

She tried to focus on her game. She was leaning over the table, when she sensed a presence behind her.

"Hey, there." A hand landed on her ass.

Brynn swiveled.

The guy was big and burly, with a bushy beard, and glassy eyes that said he'd had a few too many beers. A red, plaid shirt stretched over his wide shoulders.

"Hands off, big guy," she warned.

"But this sweet ass is begging for attention."

Ugh. She smiled sweetly. "Touch me again and you'll regret it."

"Oh yeah?" He puffed his chest up.

Brynn changed her grip on the pool cue. "Yeah."

Beyond the guy, she noted that someone else was sliding into the booth with Trucker. She could only see the back of his head. From here it didn't look like Nomad or Bender, but she couldn't be sure.

Dammit, this idiot would ruin her chance.

"Off you go," she said.

The big guy took a step toward her.

Rhys materialized by the pool table. He didn't say anything, just leaned against the table and kept his gaze on the mountain man.

"That your pretty boy?" the man asked.

"No, but I'm sure he could wipe the floor with you, asshole." She sniffed. "Not that I need help. I can do it myself."

"Ah, no need to fight. Give me a little taste and I'll—"

He stepped closer and she sensed Rhys tensing.

But Brynn whipped the pool cue up and caught Paul Bunyan under the chin. His head snapped back, and he grunted.

She spun the stick and hit him in the face.

Now, he howled.

"Are you done?" she asked.

He roared. "I'll kill you!"

She sighed. "Not done."

Mountain man moved, but Brynn wielded the cue like a bo staff. Two solid whacks with her makeshift staff and he bent over, groaning. Her next smack to the back broke the cue, but he went down.

Low male laughter filled the air.

She looked at Rhys.

"Remind me not to piss you off, Xena, Warrior Princess."

She glanced around and saw everyone in the bar watching her.

Except Trucker and the man with him.

They were arguing, and there was no sign of the third guest.

Damn.

Abruptly, the man with Trucker stood, and yanked a gun from under his jacket.

Brynn's chest locked. *Fuck.*

He shot Trucker.

Screams and cries broke out in the bar. Brynn ripped her weapon out of her satchel, and heard Rhys curse. He was beside her in a split second, Glock in hand.

The man faced the bar, the gun swiveling. Brynn didn't recognize the hard, craggy face. He wasn't one of the new bikers.

"Get down!" she yelled.

The man opened fire.

More shouts and screams, glass breaking. Rhys yanked her down behind the pool table.

"Stop! Police!" Jankowski's voice.

Brynn peered up. The detective had his weapon aimed at the gunman.

"Lower your weapon and—"

Quick as lightning, the gunman swiveled and fired at Jankowski.

No!

Adrenaline pumping, Brynn popped up. A bullet whizzed past her and she fired. The gunman flew back.

"Norcross!" she yelled.

"I'm on him." Rhys started toward the gunman.

Brynn leaped over a fallen stool. There was no sign of Jankowski.

Then, she spotted him lying flat on his back on the dirty, wooden floor. Blood bloomed on his shirt.

"No. *No.*" She dropped to her knees beside him. "Call 9-1-1," she yelled at the bartender.

The man nodded. "Already did."

"I need a cloth or a towel. Now!"

In seconds, she was pressing a towel against Jankowski's chest.

"Stay with me, Mike." He didn't make a sound. His eyes were open, but they were cloudy and filled with pain.

She looked over and saw Rhys had Trucker flat on the floor, as well.

"Rhys?"

"He's alive. Barely. The bullet hit his neck."

"The shooter?"

"Dead. You shot him in the heart."

Her stomach rolled. She'd think about that later.

Blood oozed between her fingers. Jankowski's blood.

"Hold on, Mike."

Then she heard the wail of sirens.

CHAPTER EIGHT

The X6's engine gunned as Vander drove toward the seedy bar in Oakland.

He was speeding, and breaking a few laws to get there. He didn't care.

His hands flexed on the wheel.

Shots had been fired.

There was an officer down.

He already knew that Brynn was okay. Rhys had called him.

But Vander needed to see for himself.

He screeched to a stop out front of the bar. There were a number of police cars and ambulances.

He watched paramedics loading a gurney into the back of one. Two uniforms and a detective saw him and waved him in.

The inside of the bar was dingy. His gaze caught on the blood on the floor, and his gut tightened.

He scanned the devastation and spotted Brynn. She

sat hunched in a chair, staring at nothing. Rhys stood close by, leaning against the wall, his arms crossed.

Vander strode across the room, and his brother caught his eye and nodded.

Vander crouched in front of her. "Hey."

Pale blue eyes full of misery met his. "Hey."

"How are you holding up?"

"Pretty crappy." She swallowed. "One of my fellow detectives got shot. Chest. He's in surgery."

"That is crap." Vander wanted to make it better, and it pissed him off that he couldn't.

"Trucker is critical, too. And I killed the gunman." Her chest hitched. "I don't even know his name." She held his gaze. "I killed someone."

He pressed a hand to her knee. "I'm sorry, baby."

"You've killed people."

"Yeah." And their faces had long-ago blurred into one.

"Does it...stop hurting?"

"No. But you remember why you did it, and accept that you can't change anything. The pain dulls."

Her lips trembled. "The dealer never showed."

Hmm. Likely Trucker was set up. "You need to switch it off for a bit now, Detective."

She looked at her hands. He saw that they'd been mostly wiped clean, but there were still remnants of blood under her nails and smears on her white tank top.

"I should go to the hospital and check on—"

"There's nothing you can do."

Her face twisted. "I hate that."

Yeah, being helpless was the worst.

Vander couldn't stand the misery on her face any longer. He rose and pulled her into his arms. Then he dropped into the chair and tugged her into his lap.

The way she curled into him made his chest tighten. She pressed her face under his chin and grabbed his hand.

He looked up. Rhys was eyeing him with a raised eyebrow.

Vander didn't give a shit that he'd get an interrogation from his brother later. All that mattered was Brynn.

Vander had always been a protector. He felt a deep need to take care of those he considered his. But this wave of... Shit, he didn't know what it was. Tenderness? It left him feeling a little unsettled.

He glanced back at Rhys. "You got an ID on the shooter?"

Rhys nodded. "I took a picture and sent it to Ace. His name is Duane Smith, goes by Bones. Member of the Blades. He's been suspected of being their assassin. Likes to shoot people in the head while they sleep."

Vander felt Brynn's fingers clench on his. He knew it would help to know the man she'd shot had been scum who'd hurt people.

"And the dealer didn't show," Vander said.

Brynn lifted her head. Her cheeks were pale, but he saw her brain ticking over. "Trucker was set up."

Vander nodded. "The dealer decided to eliminate him once and for all."

"Damn," she said.

Vander cupped her cheek. "You need to put it aside for now."

"I should go to the hospital and get an update on Mike." Her voice hitched. "He's got a girlfriend, and two kids from his first marriage. They're pretty tight."

"There's nothing you can do. You need to rest and regroup."

"I'll just keep hearing those gunshots. Seeing that guy fall. Mike's blood on my hands."

A man came through the bar's front door. Hunt's gaze fell on them and Vander noted the mix of emotions that hit the man's face: relief, surprise, shock, anger.

Hunt strode over. "Brynn, you okay?"

"Hunt."

She tried to get up, but Vander tightened his grip.

"Jankowski took a bullet," she said quietly. "I shot the gunman."

A muscle ticked in Hunt's jaw. "You did what you had to do. I already heard the witness reports. You had no choice." His green gaze hit Vander's. "Why is my cousin sitting in your lap?"

"Because."

That muscle ticked again.

"Come on, Brynn," Hunt said. "I'll take you home."

Her fingers tightened on Vander's again. He didn't stop to think. "She's coming with me."

Hunt stiffened. "No, she needs—"

"She knows what she needs," Vander said.

Brynn looked into his face. He already saw that her steel was reasserting itself. She held his gaze.

She blew out a breath. "I'm going with Vander."

Hunt bit out a curse, then speared Vander with a sharp look. "You take care of her."

Vander lifted his chin, then rose, keeping her close.

"Hunt," she said. "If you hear any news on Mike..."

Her cousin nodded. "I'll let you know."

"And don't tell Mom, or Bard, or my sisters what happened."

Hunt stared at her.

"Please. I'm...not ready yet."

Hunt released a breath. "Okay."

Vander waved goodbye to Rhys, then herded Brynn out to his X6. She sat in the passenger seat, her gaze dull.

He drove with restrained fury. He hated seeing her like this. He knew she was a cop, but he'd spare her this if he could.

He drove to the Norcross office and parked. "Come on."

He took her hand and led her into his private elevator up to his apartment. As they stepped out, she looked around. "Your lair. Wow, you let sunshine in here?"

The smartass was returning. He shot her a look.

She ran a hand along the back of his black, leather couch. "This is nice, Vander."

His place had the same industrial vibe as the office below, with wood floors and touches of black iron. His bedroom and bathroom were walled off, the kitchen was at the back, and a wall of accordion doors could be pushed back to open onto the huge roof terrace.

She wandered over to the windows. Outside, the setting sun glowed orange. The buildings of the city speared up, making it feel like his place was nestled in the middle of it all.

She gasped. "This terrace is amazing."

"Thanks."

Then she looked at her hands. "I still have Mike's blood under my nails, I—" Her chest hitched.

"Hey." He slid an arm around her. "Come on, Detective."

He led her into his guest bathroom. She looked around blankly, and he knew she was still lost in what had happened.

"Here." He flicked on the tap in the sink and pulled her hands under the water. He squirted some liquid soap on his own hands and ran them over hers.

She watched the water, silent. He really hated seeing her like this.

Noting the streaks of blood on her Harley Davidson tank top, he decided to find her a fresh shirt. "Stay here."

She nodded.

Vander hurried to his room, and snagged a T-shirt from his drawer. When he returned, she was still scrubbing her now-clean hands.

He shut off the water, then yanked her tank over her head. He studiously kept his gaze off her white, lacy bra and what it was cupping.

She jerked. "What are—?"

"Easy, Detective, I have a clean shirt for you." He helped her pull it on.

She fingered the soft, well-worn gray fabric. It had Army stenciled on the front.

"You were Delta Force," she said quietly.

"Yes. For a few years before they recruited me into Ghost Ops."

"Best of the best."

He took her hand and tugged her back into the living room. He went to his built-in bar and lifted a decanter. He poured two glasses of his favorite bourbon.

She took a glass and wrinkled her nose. "I hate bourbon. My dad used to drink it."

"This is Eagle Rare. The 17-year-old."

"Sounds expensive."

"It is. Drink up, Sullivan."

She gulped and pulled a face. The haunted look returned.

"I keep running through it all. Every step. Jankowski called out. Why didn't the gunman run? I saw Mike go down. Hell, I heard a bullet whizz past me."

Vander's hand curled around his glass. He hadn't heard that part. She'd almost been shot.

"It all happened so fast." She rubbed her temple.

"There's no point reliving it." He knew that better than anyone. "Would you pull the trigger again?"

She looked at him for a beat. "Yes."

"Then that's it."

"God, I hope Mike pulls through."

She looked so shattered and tired. He took her glass and his, and set them down on the coffee table. Then he pulled her down on his couch.

He lay back and pulled her down so she was stretched out, her long length pressed against him.

She leaned into him and he heard her sigh.

"Right here, I feel like nothing can get to me."

Vander pressed his cheek to her hair. He would damn well make sure that was true.

BRYNN WOKE WRAPPED AROUND A HARD, male body, her nose pressed into the skin at Vander's neck.

Mmm. Her belly flip-flopped and she realized she'd be happy to wake up like this more often.

She turned that thought over in her head, listening to his steady breathing and the solid thump of his heart under her cheek.

Vander was dangerous and complicated. And she suspected his demons ran deep.

But she wanted him. She wanted to dance with the darkness.

She noted the early morning light leaking around the blinds. Oh, boy, she'd slept with Vander Norcross, minus what she knew would be the exciting bit. Heat coiled in her belly.

She wanted that bit, too. She wanted to see if he'd let go of that legendary control.

She wanted to see all of him. Not just what he showed the world.

"How are you feeling?"

Of course, he was awake. She savored that deep rumble. "Pretty good, considering." She lifted her head and met those dark-blue eyes. "You make a very comfortable bed, Norcross."

His hand slid up to cup her hip. "Glad to hear it."

She nuzzled his throat and felt him tense. And when she heard that steady heartbeat trip, it made her giddy. "I wanted to say thank you." His skin was a little salty, and she wanted to bite him.

"You don't have to thank me."

"I know, but having you there helped. I've never taken a life before and knowing you understood helped."

His hands clamped on her harder. "I checked my phone earlier. There was a message from Hunt. Jankowski pulled through his surgery."

Her pulse skittered. "Thank God."

Vander moved, sliding her up to sit on the couch.

"The guest bathroom is through there." He pointed to a doorway. "I'll make you some coffee."

He rose, and she realized that he was avoiding her. She should be insulted, but she got the distinct impression he was fighting to keep his distance.

"Thanks."

In the bathroom—which she hadn't paid much attention to the night before—she took in the modern and masculine décor of slate gray with touches of warm wood. She found a spare toothbrush in the cabinet. She washed her face, brushed her teeth, then finger combed her hair and tied it up. She'd have to borrow Vander's T-shirt since she had zero desire to put her blood-stained tank top back on.

When she headed back out, he was in the kitchen. It was at the end of the long, large space, separated from the living area by a large dining table. The kitchen was kick-ass, with a large, black-marble island and fancy appliances.

Still, the huge terrace was the best part of his place, though.

She wondered what his bedroom looked like.

Dangerous thoughts, but Brynn had already decided. She wanted Vander Norcross, and she knew he wanted her, but was holding himself back.

Yesterday proved—in stark black-and-white—that life could be terrifyingly short. She'd first learned that as a young girl, being told her father, her hero, was never coming home.

Sometimes, you had to grab life by the horns.

She'd prefer to regret trying, than regret never taking a chance.

The scent of coffee filled the air. *Yum.* "God, caffeine."

He'd changed while she was in the bathroom and was wearing jeans, and a black T-shirt that molded over his muscular chest. And Lord help her, his feet were bare. She bit back a whimper.

He poured coffee into a mug. "Cream, two sugars."

Exactly how she liked it. "You're good."

"I am a private investigator."

She looked at the mug but didn't reach for it. She walked around the island until their bodies pressed together.

Yep, as expected, he went stiff.

"And you should be very aware that I'm attracted to you," she said.

"Brynn—"

She slid her hands up his chest. "And you're attracted to me."

"When I want a woman, I go after her, not the other way around. We are *not* doing this."

Ooh, she guessed that cool, disinterested tone was supposed to leave her bleeding.

But she felt the coiled tension in that fine, fine body of his. Felt that his heart was beating a little faster.

Because of her.

She slid one hand down to splay on his hard belly. So, so hard. She tilted her head back and met his turbulent, dark eyes.

They stared at each other.

"Damn you, Brynn." He set the mug down with a click, grabbed her, and lifted her.

She gasped and found herself seated on the cool stone of the island.

He shoved her legs apart, stepped between them and pulled her close. Their bodies were flush. Then his hungry mouth was on hers.

Yes. Everything in her came to life, electric and hot.

She wrapped her legs around his lean hips and kissed him back. He was hard and heavy against her. His kiss was raw and demanding.

She rubbed against him and felt his hard cock between her legs. She moaned into his mouth.

He deepened the kiss, tongue sliding against hers.

Oh, boy, she was a goner. The man could *kiss*.

He slid a hand under her borrowed shirt and touched her skin. She jerked and pulled him closer.

She was aware of everything: the feel of his body, his scent, his taste, the hard press of his fingers on her skin.

She wasn't thinking of who he was, or his reputation, she was only thinking of the hot man driving her out of her mind.

His mouth left hers, cruising along her jaw. "The first moment I saw you in Hunt's office..."

Her belly clenched twice as tight. "The first moment I laid eyes on that hard body of yours."

His mouth took hers again. It wasn't gentle, not a seduction. It was a full-on conquest. Luckily, she was happy to be conquered.

"*Vander.*" She writhed against him.

There was a hollow gnawing ache inside her.

"God, I think I could come just from your kisses," she panted.

The muscles in his arms tensed, and suddenly, he pulled back.

Brynn almost cried out. She watched his face shut down.

Damn. The warm feeling in her belly fizzed away.

"Was it me saying your name, or the bit about me coming?" she asked.

Vander dragged in a deep breath. "This isn't going any further."

"You keep saying that, but then you keep kissing me." *And rushing to my side, taking care of me.*

A muscle ticked in his jaw and his fingers flexed on her.

Brynn smiled. "You want me so badly you can't think straight."

He looked at the ceiling. "Christ, you really are trouble."

She stroked the hard line of his jaw. "I think you could do with a little trouble in your life."

Suddenly, he froze and his head jerked up. He looked

past her, and she heard a sound. She looked over her shoulder.

A small crowd was staring at them, including Rhys, Easton, and Gia Norcross, Saxon Buchanan, Ace Oliveira, and women that Brynn assumed were partners of the men.

There was a pretty brunette with big eyes, a grinning blonde, and a striking, pregnant woman with short, dark hair.

But it was Gia Norcross—small and curvy—who stepped forward. "Well, well. You'd better introduce us, Vander."

Brynn shifted to get off the counter.

Vander gripped her. "Don't you dare move." He kept her pinned, and she registered the very hard bulge in his jeans. She'd been happily grinding against it. Oops.

Right. She glanced back at the crowd and waved. "Hi."

Vander growled.

CHAPTER NINE

"We'll meet you downstairs." Vander shot his siblings and best friend a look they knew well.

Rhys and Easton grabbed their women. Ace and Maggie grinned. Gia looked like she was going to argue, but Saxon dragged her back down the stairs.

Hell, Vander hadn't even heard them until the last minute. He'd been too wrapped up in Brynn.

He never let anyone sneak up on him.

When he finally had his unruly cock somewhat under control, he stepped back.

Brynn ran a hand down her ponytail and grabbed her discarded coffee mug. She drank some and moaned.

Nope, cock not under control.

"I guess I'd better go," she said.

Excellent idea. He needed to clear his head.

She slid off the island. She was still in those tight jeans...

Eyes off her ass, Norcross.

"Come on." He tucked his shirt in and found her shoes. He could shower after he dealt with the gang.

They headed downstairs to the office.

The women were all draped on the couches, heads together. Even his normally 'one of the boys' helicopter pilot had gotten dragged into the girl gang. Maggie did look happy, though, so Vander couldn't complain.

"So, I'm Gia." His sister sprang up, hand outstretched to Brynn. "Vander's sister."

"I know." Brynn smiled and shook Gia's hand. "I'm Brynn. Detective Brynn Sullivan."

There were gasps from the women. Vander looked at the ceiling.

"You're a cop?" Gia breathed. "Oh, I love this!"

"We aren't together," Vander growled.

"Really?" Haven asked with a frown, eyeing the Army T-shirt Brynn was wearing.

"She spent the night at your place," Harlow said. "You barely let anyone up there, let alone women."

Brynn cocked her head and met Vander's gaze. "Really?"

Jesus. Vander shoved his hands in his pockets.

"And you were making out on your kitchen island." Maggie had a donut in her hand and took a huge bite. "It was hot."

"Oh, you think everything is hot right now," Gia said.

"Pregnancy hormones," Maggie mumbled around her donut.

"We are not together," Vander repeated.

"Yet." Brynn winked at him.

The women all traded excited looks. Vander noticed the men all averting their gazes, grinning.

"So, did you want to see some footage I have of your people of interest from Iron Wanderers?" Ace asked.

Brynn snapped to attention, morphing immediately into detective mode.

Vander found it fascinating. He jerked his gaze back to Ace. *No.* No thinking she was fascinating, gorgeous, attractive, or smart. Instantly he remembered those frenzied moments on his kitchen island. The feel of her, the taste of her...

Fuck. "Let's see it."

They headed to Ace's office. Brynn was one step behind him, followed by Rhys, Easton, and Saxon.

"Nice set-up." Brynn scanned all the screens on the wall.

Ace smiled. "Thanks. I'm Ace."

"Brynn."

"I know." He dropped into a chair. "So, I was doing some digging around on our new MC members at the time of the shooting at the Back Corner."

Vander watched Brynn's lips firm into a flat line. He knew she was thinking about shooting the gunman and her downed man.

He wanted to touch her, but he let his fingers curl into a fist, instead.

Three photos popped up.

"Bender, Shotgun, and Nomad," Brynn said.

"I'm not sure where Shotgun was at the time of the shooting," Ace said. "But, I know where Bender was."

A picture of the tattooed biker with a big-haired, buxom blonde filled the screen.

She was *really* buxom.

"Hell," Easton muttered.

"I know," Rhys murmured. "I've never seen breasts that big."

"Her name is Cindy. She works at a brothel, where Bender spent several hours."

They watched the biker pin the woman to the wall, face buried in her cleavage.

Brynn's nose wrinkled. "It's unlikely he'd be involved with targeting Trucker, if he's spending his time getting laid."

"It could be an elaborate alibi," Vander said, "but I don't think Bender is that smart. That leaves us with Shotgun and Nomad."

Ace zoomed in on still shots of the men.

"From club gossip, Nomad spends a lot of time with the ladies as well." Brynn gripped the back of a chair. "But Nomad and Bender were talking with Trucker when they set the meet at the Back Corner. Still, I can't one hundred percent rule out Shotgun. It could be either of them. From my limited interaction with them, Shotgun is smarter, and older. Nomad appears to be your typical biker with a dash of charm. He wants to ride, work on his bike, party, hang out with his brothers and get laid. He's always smiling, but it covers some intensity." She shook her head. "I can't prove anything yet."

Her cell phone rang.

"I need to take this." She stepped out. "Sullivan."

Easton straightened. "I like your woman, Vander. Tough, smart, and beautiful."

"She's not mine," Vander said.

"You look at her like she is," Rhys noted. "And you held her all snuggled up on your lap after the shooting."

"Really?" Easton said.

Saxon just smiled.

"She...tests my control," Vander conceded unhappily.

Easton gripped Vander's shoulder. "Good. We all need that sometimes. You, most of all."

"It's dangerous. I don't need it. My life is exactly how I like it." How he'd carefully crafted it.

Saxon laughed.

Vander scowled at his best friend.

"Vander, you've watched all of us have our lives— which were what we *thought* we wanted—tipped sideways by our women," Saxon said.

"And upside down," Easton said.

"Try spun around and around until nothing looked the same," Ace added dryly.

"I need things how they are." Vander glanced at the doorway. "Caring for someone...I worry about what that might unleash in me."

There. His biggest fear was on the table.

These men knew him. Knew everything he'd seen, done, waded through.

He knew he was darker, more intense, and more dangerous than anyone he knew. He needed his tight leash.

If he loved a woman... There was nothing he wouldn't do to keep her safe.

Kill. Fight. Burn the world to the ground.

He dragged in a breath. It was a risk a man like him couldn't take.

"You get to have a life, Vander," Easton said. "You've earned it, more than anyone I know. You don't have to be in protector mode all the time."

Vander shrugged. "It's the only mode I have."

"We want you to be happy," Saxon said. "We've found it, and I promise you, it's worth it."

Vander gritted his teeth, his gut churning. He wanted things he knew he couldn't have.

"Just drop it," he growled.

He saw them all trade glances.

"Okay," Easton said.

"I have some more intel on the Wanderers," Ace said, after a long moment. "It's going to be a mess there, with Trucker out of action."

Work. That's what Vander needed. There were always assholes and bad guys to keep him busy.

Vander shifted closer to Ace. "Show me."

"YES, I'M FINE. THANKS, LIEUTENANT."

Brynn ended her call with Lieutenant Cook. He'd been checking in on her.

She looked up and saw the group of beautiful women looking at her.

Based on her background checks on the Norcross family, and Hunt's input, she knew the tall, pregnant brunette with short hair was helicopter pilot Maggie

Lopez. The bombshell blonde was Harlow Carlson. The pretty, slender brunette was Haven McKinney. And the small, curvy woman with her hand on one hip was Gia Norcross.

Brynn could definitely tell that Gia was a Norcross. She had Norcross written all over her attractive face.

"So, a police detective," Gia said. "I never pictured my brother with a cop."

"Why?" Brynn asked. "Because he doesn't follow the rules?"

Gia nodded. "It's the thing I love about him. That he forges ahead and makes his own path. And it's the thing that scares me the most about him."

"Oh, I know he bends the rules, but if he ever breaks them, I'll be watching."

"Vander in handcuffs." Harlow held up a hand. "Give me a second."

Hell, Brynn needed a second as well.

"He's too scary for me," Haven said.

Maggie made a scoffing sound. "Like Rhys isn't scary."

"I know, but he smiles. He has light inside of him, as well as the dark." Haven cocked her head at Brynn. "But you're not afraid of Vander, are you?"

Brynn rocked back on her heels. These women would be a lot of help in the interrogation room. "No. I can see he's dangerous, but I'm not afraid of him."

A wide smile crossed Gia's face. "I think you might be good for my far-too-intense brother. He's used to people scrambling out of his way, or jumping at his orders."

"I've no plans to do either." Brynn had some good friends—fellow cops, a friend who was now a DEA agent —but girls' nights out and lunch dates were rare. They all worked crazy hours, and were dedicated to their careers. She considered the women in front of her. When it came to the man she was totally fascinated by, she needed all the help she could get. "He's attracted to me, I'm attracted to him, but he's holding back."

Almost as one, the women leaned closer.

Gia nodded. "I'm not surprised. He's always been intense and private. He can stand in the middle of a crowd and still be alone. And after the military..." A sad look crossed Gia's face. "It hardened him."

"He's never had a woman at his place," Harlow said.

Gia's head bobbed. "Oh, yes. He's my brother—" she pulled a face "—and I know he hooks up, but he always goes elsewhere. He never spends the whole night, and never has anyone in his loft."

"Really?" A kernel of warmth flared in Brynn's belly. She liked that. Too much. "We didn't *sleep* sleep together. I mean we slept, but that was all. He...looked after me after things yesterday. We snuggled and slept on the couch."

The women all blinked.

"Snuggled?" Gia said. "Vander snuggled?"

"And looked after you?" Maggie rubbed her small baby bump. "Like not just the 'shoot someone for you' kind of looking after you?"

Brynn nodded.

"God, I love this." Harlow clapped her hands together.

"Me too," Haven agreed.

"Me three," Gia echoed.

"He's fighting this thing pretty hard." Brynn smiled. "But I'm planning to seduce him."

"I *really* like that," Maggie said.

Gia caught Brynn's gaze and nodded.

Suddenly, Vander strode out of Ace's office.

"It's a mess at the Iron Wanderers," he said.

Brynn nodded, switching from girl talk to work. "I expected it would be. I'll know more once I take the temperature of the club."

Vander's dark brows snapped together. "You're going back there?"

"Yes. I have to finish my job. I can't close my case until I uncover the new dealer and take him down."

"It's too dangerous."

"I know it's dangerous. I'll be careful."

"Someone could have IDed you from the bar."

"We did our best to keep a lid on things. It's understandable I'd be questioned by the police. My cover should hold."

"Should?" He shook his head. "It's too risky. The dealer could know you're a cop."

"It's worth the risk."

"No. It's too dangerous and you can't go back."

Brynn stepped closer to him. "Are you enjoying that little fantasy world?"

His scowl deepened. "What?"

"The one where you issue orders and I follow them?"

"Brynn—" His voice was a dark growl.

She heard stifled laughter behind her.

"God, she's perfect for him," someone whispered. She thought it was Harlow's voice.

"Totally." That was Gia.

"Vander, I appreciate—" Brynn's phone rang. She yanked it out. "It's Hunt."

She saw Vander straighten.

"Hunt," she said.

"Where are you?"

"The Norcross Security office."

"Look, your informant called. She's totally panicked. The Iron Wanderers are in disarray. And Trucker is still unconscious in the hospital. All kinds of players are vying to take charge. Grill, the new members."

"Our dealer might out himself," she said.

"Yeah. Tonya is scared. She said tempers are running hot."

"Okay, look I need to swing home, and shower and change."

"You haven't been home?" Hunt's voice was not happy.

"Hunt, we have bigger problems right now. Are you at headquarters?"

"Yeah."

"I'll see you soon. We'll make a plan."

"Okay, Brynn."

She shoved the phone back in her pocket and looked at Vander.

"You're going to the clubhouse," he said, his voice emotionless.

"Things are a mess. It's my chance to flush out our guy."

Vander's face shut down. "Right."

Her chest tightened. She suddenly realized Vander didn't like his people being in danger. He could handle the fear, but not the fact that he couldn't control the situation.

But he had to accept that she could handle herself.

"I'm not going in half-cocked," she told him. "I'm going to talk it over with Hunt." She leaned closer, conscious of their audience. "I've got this. Any sign things are going bad, I'm out of there."

His gaze stayed locked on hers.

"I have your number. If I need extra backup, I'll call."

"It's not my business," he said stiffly.

Ouch. That hurt. She could tell he was trying to freeze her out.

What the hell happened to you, Vander?

"Too bad. I'll still call." She waved to the crowd. "Bye."

"Bye, Brynn."

"See you later."

Vander's eyes were cool. "Goodbye, Detective."

CHAPTER TEN

Vander finished eating his very excellent grilled sole with capers, and set his knife and fork down.

Business lunches were never his favorite thing, but eating with one of Norcross Security's largest clients, in his penthouse atop the 181 Freemont building, was no hardship.

He just wished he was in a better mood to appreciate Oliver Ashby's company, and the 180-degree views across the Bay.

His gaze swung to the Bay Bridge and beyond to Oakland. Was Brynn back at the Wanderers clubhouse? His gut cramped in a way that it hadn't since his first Ghost Ops mission.

"I can't thank you enough, Vander. Ace's work with my system security team was top-notch."

Oliver was a trim, sixty-two-year-old businessman. His mostly gray hair topped a broad, handsome face. He wore a Rolex on his wrist, and a pressed shirt tucked into his tailored pants.

He looked exactly like what he was—a wealthy, successful businessman who built his company, Binary Tech, from the ground up.

"It's always a pleasure to help you, Oliver." Vander gave the man a faint smile. "Norcross Security is always happy to work with you."

"And send me a big bill," Oliver said good-naturedly.

"That, too." Vander looked out the window again. Was Brynn okay?

Oliver laughed, then his face turned serious. "And I appreciate your personal help with the other matter, as well."

That more delicate matter was a claim by a twenty-five-year-old man that he was Oliver's abandoned love child, and therefore entitled to his millions.

Vander had done some digging. The young man was born and raised in Iowa to farmer parents. It turned out he'd been hired by Oliver's bitter ex-wife to cause him grief. Oliver was now—happily—married to wife number three. Wife one had been a childhood sweetheart, and the mother of his adult children. She'd died of cancer a decade ago. Wife number two had been what Oliver liked to call his ill-advised midlife crisis. At the time, she'd been a gorgeous, twenty-eight-year-old super-model. After their short marriage and divorce, she'd blown through her generous settlement, and still plagued him.

"Would you gentlemen like a drink?" Oliver's current wife, Alicia, entered the room. She slid an arm across her husband's shoulders and sat on the arm of his chair. "Coffee, whiskey? Vander, I know you enjoy a good bourbon."

Vander shook his head. "Not for me, Alicia. Thank you."

The woman was a beautiful, well-groomed blonde in her forties. She owned a successful therapy practice.

She cocked her head. "You seem...off today, Vander."

He controlled the urge to shift in his chair. "I have a lot on my mind."

"You need to relax." Alicia smiled. "I have a lovely lady who works for me. Attractive, sweet. Maybe I could give you her number?"

"No, thanks." His voice was a little more forceful than he'd intended.

Oliver smiled, tightening his arm around his wife. "Something tells me Vander already has his eye on someone. I recognize the look."

Vander sipped his water and stayed silent.

Alicia tilted her head and studied Vander's face. "But she isn't making it easy."

"Good," Oliver said. "You made me work for it." The couple smiled at each other. "It was the best thing I ever did."

"Aw." She kissed him.

"I'm not the relationship type," Vander told them.

"Bullshit," Oliver disagreed. "We all are. The love of a good woman makes a man."

Alicia nodded. "It doesn't matter where we've been, or what we've been through, Vander, we all deserve love."

Jeez, everyone was giving romance lectures lately.

"Not me." He rose, setting his napkin on the table. "Like I said, always a pleasure."

Oliver nodded. He and Alicia stood as well, and the

businessman shook Vander's hand. "I'll see you next time."

Vander headed down in the elevator and then into the lobby. As he strode out, a tall blonde with killer cleavage in a fitted skirt and blouse caught his gaze. She spotted him, her steps slowing.

He ignored the invitation in her eyes and strode past her.

All he could see were crystal-blue eyes and a sprinkle of maddening freckles.

Outside the building, he checked his phone. She'd said she'd call if she needed help.

Would she? Brynn Sullivan would probably be under fire in a sinking boat being circled by sharks before she'd concede that she needed help.

He blew out a breath. She'd needed help after the shooting. She'd needed him then.

She'd leaned on him, slept in his arms.

Fuck.

He headed down the street to where he'd parked his bike. He'd check in with Ace. See if anything was going down at the Wanderers clubhouse. Hell, he'd even call Hunt and find out exactly where Brynn was.

"Hello, there."

The feminine purr made him whirl. It was the blonde from the lobby. She was toying with her necklace, no doubt to draw attention to her cleavage.

"Hi." He started to turn away, but she grabbed his arm.

"I saw you back there." She smiled, and artfully

nibbled on her bottom lip. "I'm intrigued. You totally rock a suit."

"Look, I—"

She stepped closer, pressing her breasts against him. "I have an apartment in the building. I'd really like to ride your cock."

His eyebrows winged up. He'd had his share of aggressive sexual offers since he'd hit his teens, but this was topping the list.

Her hand pressed to his abs and slid south.

"Maybe you'd let me suck you first? I'm good with my mouth. And I have some silk ropes if you want to tie me up."

Alarm bells rang in his head. Something was off. Way off.

He grabbed her wrist and twisted her hand away from him. She gasped.

"Who put you up to this?" he demanded.

Fear filled her eyes, confirming his suspicions.

"No one, I—"

Vander leaned in and lowered his voice. "Who. Hired. You?"

The come-hither look faded. "Some biker. He told me where you'd be, and to stall you. To keep you busy for a few hours." Her gaze raked him. "If I knew what you looked like, I would've given him a discount."

"Name?" Vander clipped.

Her chin lifted. "We didn't trade names."

Vander shoved her away from him. *Fuck.* This meant trouble.

Brynn was in trouble.

Before he reached his bike, his phone rang. "Norcross."

There was a pause. "Ah, Norcross, this is Badger."

One of his informants. Badger worked the streets, had no real allegiance to anyone. He was quiet and unassuming, and got close enough to see things because no one paid him much attention.

"Badger, I'm —"

"It's your woman."

"My woman?" Tension crept into Vander's muscles.

"Yeah. The pretty brunette with all the colors in her hair. Working with the Wanderers."

Brynn. "What about her?"

There was an audible swallow. "Something's going down. The Wanderers think she's a snitch. She's in danger, man."

Fuck.

"Thanks, Badger."

Vander ended the call and ran for his bike.

BRYNN STACKED parts in the Wanderers garage, and every now and then, she glanced over at the clubhouse.

There'd been people coming and going the last few hours. She'd witnessed one heated argument between Nomad and Grill.

She pretended to tinker with a half-pulled-apart bike. She really wanted to get into the clubhouse, but there was no way they'd let her in.

She'd seen her informant, Tonya, and some of the

other old ladies earlier, but the woman had hurried off with a nervous look.

Brynn blew out a breath. She could feel the undertone of violence. Something was brewing, and it wasn't going to be long before it all spilled over.

Hunt and a group of cops were waiting to swoop in... once she knew the identity of the dealer. But at this point, she still had nothing.

An older member, Baz, sauntered out of the clubhouse. He wore a leather vest over his denim shirt, and had a thin, scraggly beard. He was shaking his head. He spotted her and angled her way.

"Hey, Baz." He was one of the decent members of the club.

"Girl, I suggest you get gone. Things are heating up in there." He shook his head again. "If Trucker was here, he'd be pissed as hell."

"How's he doing?"

"He's in a coma or something." Baz stroked his beard. He looked troubled. "Someone said you were there."

Crap. She'd hoped that she'd flown completely under the radar. "I was shooting some pool. Then the real shooting started. I crawled under a table."

"You don't look like life has worn you down yet. This life has its good moments, but I'm not sure this is a place for you."

"What's going on in there?" She tipped her head toward the clubhouse.

Baz let out a noisy breath. "They're all squabbling for control. Trucker isn't even in a grave yet. Ain't right."

"Isn't Grill next in line?"

"That boy's crazy. He's not fit to run the club."

"The new guys?"

Baz scowled. "Haven't proven themselves yet. Some are a bit too fucking full of themselves."

"Oh?"

"Yeah, I—" He broke off and shook his head. "It's club business. You should get out of here, Bry. Until the dust settles."

"I'm nearly finished with these parts, then I'll head off. Thanks, Baz."

He gave her a chin lift, then ambled over to his Harley.

The engine growled to life and he pulled out.

Brynn decided to hang around until someone else came out, and then she'd see if she could get a feel for what was happening.

She wiped her hands on a rag. She was in jeans again today, with a cute, mechanic-style shirt with a patch on it that had a logo for a brand of oil. Carrin had bought it for her.

Suddenly, the door of the clubhouse opened. A group of members sauntered out. None looked happy.

They didn't even look her way before jumping on their bikes and roaring off.

Damn. Her gut told her she wasn't going to find out anything useful today. She might as well head to the hospital to check on Jankowski. She'd take him a box of the Krispy Kremes she was always giving him hell for loving.

The clubhouse door opened again and Grill stalked out, practically vibrating with fury. Brynn shrank back into the shadows. He leaped on his bike, shot a steaming glare at the clubhouse, then rode off.

It looked like whatever had happened, Grill hadn't gotten what he wanted.

She made herself busy stacking parts. She'd see who came out next, then she'd leave.

Finally, the door opened, and Nomad walked out, flanked by two enforcers she didn't know.

A prickle skittered across the back of her neck.

Gone was the wide, flirtatious smile. His lean face looked harder, and even across the courtyard, she sensed a sharpness to his gaze.

Brynn had a gut deep instinct she knew who the new dealer was.

And he'd been playing them the entire time.

He lifted his gaze and it locked on hers.

He stared at her for a second, then started her way, the two bikers following.

Her pulse kicked up a notch, and she made sure it didn't show. Her fingers tightened on the wrench in her hand.

"Bry," Nomad drawled.

That storm she'd sensed brewing had arrived.

"Nomad, how are things? How's Trucker?"

"You would know, wouldn't you?"

She raised her brows. "Baz said he's in a coma."

"Oh, but I'm sure you've had regular updates from your friends in blue."

Brynn made herself blink. "My friends in blue?"

"Yes. Heard you're tight with the cops. All cozy with them at the Back Corner after the shooting."

"I talked with them—"

"Yes. I think you talk with them a lot."

Shit. It didn't sound like he knew she was a cop, but it was clear he suspected something.

"You think I'm a snitch?" She gave him a belligerent look. "You just got to San Francisco, what would you know?"

"I'm new to town, but I'm not new to snitches." He nodded, and the two bikers stepped forward, their faces stony.

Neither of them looked like they'd mind roughing up a woman. *Crap. Crap. Crap.*

"So, what? You're taking over, and what you say goes?" She slid her hand into her back pocket and found her phone. She'd programmed Vander's number for a quick dial and she pressed the button.

"Yes," Nomad said.

So, Nomad was the dealer.

He spread out his hands. "We're expanding the Iron Wanderers operations."

"Trucker won't be happy," she said.

"Trucker won't be breathing. And you won't talk. Especially if your jaw is wired shut."

Fuck this asshole. "I'm trembling."

"Teach her a lesson, boys."

The first biker came at her, lazy and relaxed, like she was a fly that needed swatting.

Brynn braced, then released a slow, controlled breath.

Then she leaped up and swung her wrench with all her strength.

It collided with the man's jaw, making a sickening crunch.

She didn't stop. She whirled again, and just managed to duck a punch from the second biker.

"Thee broke my thaw," the guy on the ground cried.

She stayed focused on her second attacker. He swung at her again and she ducked and weaved. She was well-trained, but he was bigger and stronger, with hands like bricks.

She got a kick in to his gut, and heard him grunt.

"Bitch!" With a snarl, he came at her.

His next hit caught her in the ribs, driving her into a bench. Pain sparked like a flare. She reached out and grabbed a hammer off the bench. She swung wide and caught him in the face. He staggered and fell.

Brynn leaped on top of him, driving him to the dirty, concrete floor. She grabbed his head, and rammed it into the ground.

His eyes rolled back in his head, and his body sagged. He was out.

The blow to her face caught her by surprise.

Pain exploded and she felt Nomad's knuckles grind against her lips. She slipped, flew sideways, and hit the floor.

"I'm going to teach you a lesson, pretty little snitch." He landed a vicious kick to her side, right where her ribs were already sore. She groaned through the pain.

Get up. If she didn't move, she was dead.

Brynn scrambled away and slid her hand into her boot.

She yanked her knife from where she kept it hidden. She'd paid a fortune for the sleek, little sheath.

Nomad kept coming at her.

She slashed at him and heard him curse. Blood ran down his forearm.

Then, while he was distracted, she lunged at him again and swung the knife a second time.

He swiveled at the last minute, but the blade still sank into his shoulder.

He bellowed. "You'll pay for that, you bitch."

Then he reached back and pulled a handgun from the waistband of his jeans.

Oh. *Shit.*

Time moved in slow motion, her brain assessing the situation in small flashes.

She noted the gun. That she had no time to run. That Vander was too far away to help. Thoughts of her mom, and her siblings hit her.

And Vander.

The man she hadn't had a chance with.

A chance she'd really wanted.

Suddenly, the roar of a bike engine brought the world back into real time.

Vander's black BMW roared right into the garage.

He leaped off it.

The bike skidded and crashed into Nomad, knocking him down.

Then Vander leaped on Brynn, taking her to the floor.

CHAPTER ELEVEN

Vander pushed himself up, and pulled Brynn up with him.

He noted the swelling and the start of the bruising on her face. His jaw locked.

He pulled his Glock and swiveled. He lifted the gun and advanced on Nomad, stepping over the still bodies of the other unconscious bikers.

Nomad was still cursing and righting himself. He spotted Vander and his eyes went wide. He dived under a workbench.

Vander fired, but couldn't see the asshole. "Brynn?"

"Here. I'm okay."

Her voice was right behind him. She was sticking close.

A flash of movement. Vander swiveled and fired again.

He heard a yelp. A dash of movement behind another bench. Then a second later, Nomad sprinted out of the garage door toward the clubhouse, yelling.

The doors of the clubhouse burst open and bikers spilled out.

Armed bikers.

Fuck. Vander spun. "Time to go."

Her eye was already swelling. Anger—dark and deadly—shot through him, but he locked it down.

"Help me." He pressed his ass against the bike's seat, then bent his legs. He pushed up and Brynn heaved with him. They got the bike upright, then he climbed on and waved at her. She threw her leg over and settled behind him.

Vander gunned the engine, and they roared out of the garage. She pressed close to his back, her arms clamped around him.

As they sped onto the street, Brynn shifted, yelling against the wind.

"We have company!"

Vander heard the throaty growl of lots of bikes. He looked back and saw the gang of Harleys spilling onto the street to chase them.

Shit.

"Gun," she snapped.

He reached down and pulled the Glock out. He handed it back to her.

She took it, and a second later, pressed a hand to his shoulder and twisted back.

She fired evenly spaced shots.

Vander glanced back and saw Harleys swerving. One crashed into a parked car.

Two bikes swerved and collided with each other, the riders spilling onto the road.

But more kept coming.

"Hold on," he roared.

Brynn sat, tightening her grip. He turned and they raced toward the bridge.

Several Harleys drew closer. Brynn fired again.

The traffic thickened. Vander weaved in and out of the cars.

Suddenly, a Harley sped out of the side street ahead of them.

Shit. It was Grill.

The biker pulled a huge handgun.

"Brynn!" Vander yelled.

"I see him."

Grill fired at them, and Vander dodged.

"I'm out of ammo," she cried.

"Left pocket."

He felt her reach into his pockets. Then she held on and leaned to the side.

"Hold steady," she said.

She fired on Grill.

The biker ducked and weaved. Several cars screeched to a stop, and Vander avoided them.

The bridge loomed ahead.

Vander's BMW was at least seventy or eighty miles per hour faster than the Harley. If they could get out of this traffic, he could lose the bikers.

He accelerated. The BMW shot forward, moving fast. Brynn fired on Grill again.

The biker jerked to the side, and narrowly missed hitting a car.

She fired again.

Grill flew off his Harley. He went one way, and his bike went another.

A delivery truck crashed into the bike with a loud crunch of metal. The truck slammed on its brakes.

"Hold on tight," Vander told her.

She tucked herself against his back and clamped on.

Vander accelerated. He focused on the road as they raced across the bridge.

He risked a glance back. No bikers were giving chase, and they couldn't catch them now, regardless.

But that didn't mean that Nomad, or the Wanderers, would give up. The Iron Wanderers were known for a culture of revenge and payback. Especially Grill.

Once they discovered that Brynn was a cop, they'd really be out for blood.

Vander didn't head for the Norcross Security office. He needed to get the lay of the land first.

Eventually, they crossed into San Francisco. He slowed and blended into the city traffic.

They ended up in the Embarcadero, down by the water. He slowed to a stop and swiveled. Brynn eased off the bike and Vander did the same.

He bit back a curse. Her face was a mess. Her eye was swelling, and she was going to end up with a hell of a bruise. *Assholes*. His fingers curled, but he got a lock on the rage.

Gently, he cupped her cheek and turned her face.

"You need ice." He lightly probed her cheekbone, and she winced. "I don't think it's broken."

"I'll be fine." Those big, pale-blue eyes met his. "Vander, thank you. You—"

He yanked her to his chest. Her arms wrapped around him, tight.

"I called you when I realized things had gone bad." She looked up at him. "But how did you get there so fast?"

"I was already on my way." He ran a finger down her cheek. "An informant called and told me that my woman was in danger."

"Your woman?" Their gazes stayed locked.

"I was almost there when your call came in. I broke the speed limit to reach you."

If he'd been a minute later, she'd be dead. His hands flexed on her. Nomad would have killed her.

"This time, I'm glad you broke the rules." She leaned closer. "I'm all right, Vander."

Fuck, she stirred things in him. He forced himself to let her go, and pulled out his phone. He rang Saxon.

"You all right?" his best friend asked.

"Yeah. I take it that it's all over the news?"

"Shots fired at the Iron Wanderers clubhouse. High-speed bike chase in Oakland. Yeah. How's Brynn?"

"She's with me. She's a little battered, but okay."

"I'm fine," she said.

Vander ignored her.

"Does she need medical attention?" Saxon asked. "I can call Ryder."

"I need to take a look first. If her injuries are bad enough, then yeah, we'll call Ryder."

Brynn gasped. "Don't call my cousin. He'll lose it."

"Hang on," Saxon said. "Ace has something. I'm putting you on speaker."

"Vander." Ace's voice. "It's everywhere. The Wanderers want you and Brynn, dead or alive. They've put a price on you both."

"Is Nomad insane?" Brynn asked. "Putting a bounty on Vander Norcross and a cop?"

"Nomad wants to make a name for himself." Vander narrowed his gaze. "He'll regret it."

"Vander, he's calling in all the Wanderers' markers," Ace said. "Allied biker clubs, gangs like the Blades. He's flooding San Francisco with assholes looking for the two of you."

Fuck. "Lock down the office, Saxon. Coordinate with Hunt."

Brynn's cheeks paled. "My family. My mom—"

Crap, she was right. "Tell Hunt to get security on Brynn's family. Same for mine. Send Rome to watch my parents. Lock Gia and the women down."

"Okay, I'll take care of it." Saxon's tone was dark. "Vander, you and Brynn need to lay low until we have a plan of attack to handle this."

Dammit. "I'll take care of it." He met Brynn's gaze. He'd take care of her. *No one* was hurting her. "I'll be in touch."

"Be careful, Vander," Saxon said.

BRYNN HELD onto Vander as he rode toward a warehouse in the Embarcadero.

Her face was starting to hurt. It was throbbing, and the skin felt tight. Her ribs ached as well.

The small warehouse was brick, and wedged between two larger ones. Her belly was tied up in knots, knowing that there was a bounty on both hers and Vander's heads.

God. Hunt would be furious.

Brynn felt bad. She'd dragged Vander into this mess.

She saw him reach down and touch his phone. The large sliding door on the warehouse opened and he rode inside.

Lights clicked on and Brynn gasped.

The door slid shut behind them.

The warehouse had a polished-concrete floor. Gleaming cars and motorbikes lined both sides of the space. Some looked modern and new; others looked like collectibles. A large turntable was set in the floor in the center of the space, so there was no awkward reversing in and out.

Other vehicles were stored up on hoists near the roof.

Vander turned off the bike's engine and set the kickstand down.

"Wow doesn't seem to do this place justice," she said. "Is it yours?"

"Yeah. It's not listed under my name, so no one can track us here very easily."

She scanned around. "Boys and their toys."

Strong fingers lightly gripped her chin. "You need ice." He probed her cheek again and she winced. "And some painkillers, I'm guessing."

"I wouldn't say no."

Darkness moved through his gaze. He stroked her cheek gently. "Nomad will pay for this."

She gripped Vander's wrist. "Hey, don't forget that I'm okay."

"He hit you."

"And I stabbed him."

"I don't care. Nomad will still regret it." Vander dropped his hand and took hers. "Come on."

He led her to the back of the warehouse. Ferrari. Aston Martin. Lamborghini. Maserati. She couldn't begin to calculate what this little collection was worth.

There was a small workshop and office tucked at the back. He gestured to a chair, then fished around in a mini fridge and cupboard. He came back with an ice pack, a towel, and a first aid kit. He wrapped the towel around the ice pack.

He pressed the bundle to her cheek. "Hold that."

"Ugh, I hate having cold things pressed to my skin."

He shot her a look, then pulled various items out of the first aid kit. "It's too risky to call Ryder. Someone could trail him here. So, you'll have to make do with me." Vander handed her some pills and a water bottle. "Take these."

She obeyed. He was in the mood to take care of her, and the look on his face warned her not to argue.

"So, are we going to stay here?" she asked.

"No. It's not set up for anyone to stay here, and I won't run the risk that some asshole has seen me drive in here at some stage."

Paranoid. She wasn't surprised. "What's the plan?"

"We need to get out of town until things die down a bit. Maybe for a few days. Then I can coordinate with my team and Hunt, and we'll work out how to take Nomad down."

Oh, taking Nomad down was a plan she could totally get on board with.

"So, where will we go? We could find a cheap motel somewhere."

Dark-blue eyes met hers. "I have a cabin. It's on the way to Tahoe, a few hours' drive from here. We can stay there."

Well, he had a warehouse full of cars, so she shouldn't be surprised he also had a cabin. She looked out the doorway of the office at the sexy, red Ferrari parked close by. And his warehouse in South Beach had to have cost him a pretty penny.

"How rich are you?"

He shot her a quick smile. "I do okay. Easton invests for us."

"Must be nice having a billionaire brother. My brother is a firefighter." She nibbled her lip. "I'll have to call my mom and Bard. Explain. They'll be worried."

Vander pointed to a phone on the bench. "Use this one. It has encryption. I doubt the Wanderers have any tech-savvy members, but just in case they can trace your phone... Talk to Hunt, too. I'll put the bike away."

"We aren't going to take it to the cabin?"

"The Wanderers know what it looks like. We'll trade it for another one."

He walked out and Brynn took a second to admire the back view of him.

She really, *really* wanted to see him naked.

Soon.

This man had risked his life to rescue her. She was done letting him hold himself back.

She called Hunt first. Unsurprisingly, he was pissed.

"I'm fine. I'm with Vander."

She heard her cousin's harsh breath. "You're not injured?"

"Blow to the face and ribs, nothing's broken. Vander's given me an ice pack and pain meds. We're going to lay low for a few days."

"I'm going to talk to him. If you get hurt..."

"Can you think of a safer place for me?"

A pause. "No. Vander would die to protect you."

Her gut tied in knots. She didn't want Vander hurt or dead. She realized just how deep her feelings were getting.

He'd fight to protect her. Well, she'd fight to protect him, as well.

"I'm going to call Mom now," she said.

"I'm assigning an officer to her house."

"Carrin, Naomi, Bard—?"

"I'm on it."

Relief filled Brynn. "Thanks, Hunt. Can you check on Mom and assure her that I'm all right?"

"You know I will."

"And can you call Bard and explain? He'll hate having a bodyguard."

"Coward."

"Totally." Her brother would blow a gasket.

"I'll talk to him, and Naomi and Carrin. You just focus on you, and staying safe."

"Bye, Hunt. Love you."

"Love you too, Bee."

Brynn spoke quickly with her mom, and tried to downplay the situation. But Ellen Sullivan was a cop's wife and widow.

"Brynn Celine Sullivan, I know you aren't sharing the entire truth with me."

"Mom, I promise I'm safe."

"I hate thinking of you alone."

"Well... I'm not." She looked into the warehouse. Vander was talking on his cell phone, one hand on his hip. No doubt to Hunt. His jacket was gone and he'd rolled up his sleeves again. Did he have any idea what that did to her?

"Now, that's a tone of voice I haven't heard you use before," her mom said.

"I'm with a man. A handsome, dangerous, good, complicated man."

"Well, well." Her mom sniffed.

"Mom, you crying?"

"Of course not. He'll keep you safe?"

"Yes. And I'll keep him safe."

"Good. Tell him I expect him over for dinner after all of this is over."

"Okay, Mom." If Brynn could convince Vander to let himself off that leash he kept himself on. "I love you, Mom."

"You too, baby girl. Be safe."

The painkillers kicked in. She was checking her ribs when Vander strode back in. His brows snapped together.

"Why didn't you tell me that you were hurt some-where else?"

"Well, I—"

He jerked her shirt up.

"Hey!"

"Hold still. Goddammit, Brynn."

She looked down. Ah, the bruising was already show-ing. It was going to be a doozy. "There aren't any broken bones."

His scowl deepened. His hand splayed over her ribs.

Sensation skated over her skin and she sucked in a breath.

His gaze lifted.

Screw it. She just survived a shootout and chase. She deserved a little reward.

She went up on her toes and kissed him.

For a beat, he stayed still, then his mouth opened and he kissed her back.

Mmm. It was a deep, sexy, drugging kiss. They were both making sure the other was okay.

Then his hands tightened and he stepped back. She saw his mask slam down on his face.

"This still isn't happening," he said.

Frustration bit at her. "Vander—"

"Listen." His gaze, dark and intense, was pinned on her. There was so much churning in the depths of those eyes. "I take care of my friends, my family, the people who work for me. I do everything I can to keep them safe."

She knew that. The man was a born protector. He couldn't switch it off. It was a compulsion.

"It's why I do my bit to keep San Francisco safe. Not out of the goodness of my own heart, but for them. For the people I care about."

She nodded. She understood completely.

He leaned in, his gaze running over her face. "If I let myself care too much, fall in love..."

Her chest hitched.

"There's *nothing* I wouldn't do to keep the woman I loved safe. No line I wouldn't cross. No law I wouldn't break."

Her throat tightened. She couldn't talk, she could barely breathe.

"It's a risk I can't take. A man like me is too dangerous to fall in love."

Silence fell and he stepped back.

"Get ready. We'll head out now. The sooner we're out of the city, the better."

Then he turned and walked away.

And that's when Brynn realized that she wasn't the only one with deepening feelings.

A million butterflies took flight in her belly.

CHAPTER TWELVE

V ander gunned the Ducati Super Sport east toward Lake Tahoe.

Brynn was tucked tight behind him, and he was excruciatingly conscious of every inch of her against him.

The perfect fit.

He had decided on a different bike, rather than taking a car. It gave them more options if they needed to go off-road. It was also bright red, so no one would mistake it for his black BMW. They both also wore leather jackets and black helmets.

He'd been on edge the entire time they'd traveled through the city, knowing people were searching for them. He'd relaxed a fraction the minute they were clear of the city sprawl. All he was focused on now was getting Brynn safe. Get to his cabin, and then he could fully relax.

They continued on smaller, quieter roads, and surprisingly, he found himself enjoying the ride. She kept a firm grip on him, and leaned easily into the corners with him. Riding like she'd been on a bike all her life. She matched his moves, fully in sync. He'd never felt that way about anyone before.

He shook his head. He wasn't going there.

They passed through the small town of West Grove. It was the one closest to his place. Once they were settled, he'd come back and grab some food and supplies.

Finally, he slowed and turned off onto a smaller road. He rode deeper into the forest.

Vander thought of Nomad and the Wanderers. He ground his teeth together. Nomad had picked the wrong city to infiltrate. Vander was going to make him regret it.

He'd either send the biker back to Arizona, or kill him. Thinking about Brynn's face, the latter seemed much more appealing.

Vander turned again and rode through some stone gates. The gravel road was rough, and he slowed down before finally pulling to a stop outside his cabin.

Brynn slid off the bike and pulled her helmet off. Her hair spilled over her shoulders.

She made a choked sound. "Vander, this is *not* a cabin."

"It's a wooden house in the forest."

She snorted. "It's an architecturally designed piece of gorgeousness. Look at it."

The building was long and sleek, with a vaguely Scandinavian feel to it. Lots of wood, glass and natural stone. The windows were floor-to-ceiling panels of solid glass. There was a detached garage off to the side, where he kept his Mercedes G-class SUV.

147

He used his phone to turn off his security system, then unlocked the front door and let her in.

There was lots of natural wood, and everything was sleek and minimalist. He didn't get here often, and he wasn't one for decorating.

"It's essentially off-grid. The place has solar panels and a small wind turbine. It's owned through a series of companies, so it can't be traced back to me. I have a care-taker who lives down the road and keeps it clean."

Brynn wandered around. "Vander, this place is amazing."

Large, sliding doors led onto a wide, back deck. There was a sunken fire pit off to one side, and the deck led straight to the pond. The still surface of a decent-sized pond gleamed, surrounded by trees.

"Can you swim in there?" she asked.

He nodded. "And fish." He had fishing gear in a small, wooden storage box. Outdoor furniture was dotted around the deck—a wooden table and chairs, and wide loungers topped with cream cushions.

"It's truly gorgeous. Peaceful."

He shrugged. "I don't get here often. My family uses it sometimes, but Easton has a big place on Lake Tahoe. We usually go there for family events."

So, this was his place. His family understood his need for solitude.

"There are three guest bedrooms, so take your pick. And everyone's left a few things here over time, so you should be able to find some clothes that fit in the closets."

She nodded and wrapped her arms around herself.

"All right?" he asked.

"I guess the reality of what happened is sinking in." Her chin lifted. "I'll be fine."

Of course, she would. Brynn Sullivan was made of tough stuff.

"Let me check your face." He led her to the kitchen and she sat on a stool. "Do you need more painkillers?"

She nodded. "That's probably best."

The bruising was going to be bad. He gently stroked her cheekbone, and then got her some pills.

"I can't wait to get rid of my fake tattoos," she said.

"Not into tattoos?"

She swallowed the pills and smiled. "I have one real one."

"Where?" He hadn't spotted any.

She shot him a feminine smile that he felt in his cock. "It's a secret. I've never even told my mom."

"My mother despairs about her sons all having ink. Doesn't change how she feels about us, but she isn't a big fan. Rhys has the most, and even Easton has some."

She tilted her head. "And you? I haven't noticed any."

He smiled. "It's a secret."

Their gazes stayed locked, and he was suddenly intensely curious to know where her tattoo was.

Fuck. He looked away. "I'm going to head into town and stock up on food. Maybe find some more clothes."

Her eyebrows lifted. "On the bike?"

He smiled. "No, I have an SUV here."

"Okay, well I'm totally going to snoop around while you're gone."

"I didn't expect anything less, Detective."

"Get some chocolate, please. I think I've earned it."

"Roger that."

He headed out, but paused at the front door and looked back. She was standing by one of the large windows looking out at the pond, and he felt a punch to his gut. She looked so right there.

Vander shut that thought down fast. This would all be over soon, and she'd go back to her cop life, and he'd go back to his world among the shadows.

He pulled out his phone and texted Saxon and Hunt to let the men know that they were safe.

His phone vibrated.

Take care of my cousin, Vander, or you'll regret it.

As always, Hunt never minced his words.

Saxon messaged to say that Ace and Rhys were pulling every shred of intel they could find on the Wanderers and Tony "Nomad" Garcia.

Will email it through tonight. You and your detective get some rest today. We'll make battle plans tomorrow.

Thanks, Saxon.

Vander opened the garage, unveiling his rugged, decked-out G-class in matte black. He got in and reversed out, then headed into town.

There was a surprising and unfamiliar ache in his chest. He realized that he didn't like leaving Brynn alone. He shook his head. "She's a cop. She'd kick your ass if she knew you were thinking that."

His hands tightened on the wheel. He *had* to stop thinking about her.

All he was going to do for the next few days was feed her, tend her injuries, and keep her safe.

That was it.

Nothing else.

He turned onto the highway and headed for West Grove.

BRYNN TOTALLY SNOOPED.

She found the master bedroom at the end of the hall. There was more gorgeous, warm wood, and a sleek bed made up with gray bedding. The windows offered a perfect view of the water and trees.

She could practically feel her blood pressure lowering, standing there.

She didn't get a personal sense of Vander from the room, but she knew he was a man who didn't give much away, even when it came to his personal space. There was an awesome bathroom, with a huge, open shower, and a long, wooden vanity. The pièce de résistance was a large, freestanding stone tub that would be perfect for bubble baths.

Back in the bedroom, she spotted a small frame on a floating shelf. She picked it up, and her chest tightened.

It was Vander with a group of men. They weren't in uniform, but she knew this must've been his Ghost Ops team. He stood in the center, with his arm around Rhys, who had much shorter hair. They were all wearing cargo shorts and T-shirts. All of them were muscular and tough-looking. Vander had a faint half smile on his face, and one guy was on his knee at the front, mugging for the camera.

These men were like his brothers. Men he'd depended on in the middle of hell. Although Vander was their commander, so she knew he would have held himself a little apart. He would have felt responsible for them.

Had they all made it back? If they had, were they guarded too? Keeping themselves from truly living?

She headed back to the living area. The pain pills had kicked in, and she didn't feel any aches. She opened the sliding door and stepped onto the deck.

Nice. She breathed deep. She felt all the stress leak away...except the driving need she felt for the man she wanted more than anything.

It was just the two of them now, and for the moment, they were safe.

Brynn knew Vander's warning was real. If she went further with him, if she let herself tumble all the way in love with him, he'd be overprotective, bossy, and over-bearing.

But she also knew, deep in her gut, that he'd love so fiercely. Like nothing she'd ever felt before.

How would it feel to be the very center of Vander Norcross' universe?

Delicious heat coiled inside her. She realized she didn't have a choice. She wanted him and she was going to make him realize that what they had was too powerful to ignore.

She wanted to love him. He deserved it so much.

But first, she wanted him to let go of that strict control he held onto tightly. To feel. To live.

She watched the smooth water of the pond. It reminded her of him—still, cool, and controlled on the surface.

But she really wanted to see what was beneath.

She heard a door open and looked back. She watched as he strode in and dumped some bags on the kitchen island.

"Found everything?" she asked.

He stepped onto the deck. "Yes."

"I really like it here. It's so peaceful."

"When I come here, I sit out here for hours. Drop in a line."

"You come alone?"

He met her gaze. "That's how I prefer it."

She looked back at the pond. "Well, I think I'm going to test the water."

"There are perfectly good showers inside."

She smiled at him over her shoulder. "I know, but it's a beautiful day, and I feel like a swim."

"You don't have a swimsuit."

She grinned. "That doesn't really matter." She unbuttoned her jeans and shimmied them off. He cursed and turned away.

"Never pegged you for shy, Norcross."

She yanked her shirt off and ditched her underwear.

He didn't say anything. She looked at his broad back, and felt the tension throbbing off him.

But she noted that he didn't leave.

Brynn stepped into the water. It was nice—not cold,

but fresh and cool on her skin. She slipped in and then pushed off. She swam to the center of the pond.

"The water is great." She looked back and saw him now seated on a wooden, outdoor chair. He leaned forward, his hands steepled between his knees.

Brynn dived under and did a few laps. She liked swimming, and didn't get to do it often enough. She did a few more laps.

"You like swimming, Norcross?" she called out.

"Yeah."

She turned to face him. "You should come in."

No response.

No, he was sitting there watching her. Brooding.

God, she wanted to give him something. Ease the pain, the burden he carried. To let him feel pleasure, feel free.

They'd survived a gun fight with bikers today, and she felt very, very alive.

Brynn swam back toward the deck. She slicked her hair back.

Then she took a deep breath, absorbed her jittering nerves, and pushed out of the pond.

She stood there on the deck, water sluicing off her. For a second, she savored his intense gaze moving over her body.

Then she started toward him.

"What the hell are you doing?" he growled.

"I'm seducing you." She stopped in front of him.

"I already said that wasn't happening. I'm not interested, and you're just embarrassing yourself."

Ooh, that cold tone was designed to slice and hurt.

But she saw the way he gripped the arms of the chair. Saw his pulse pounding in his throat.

A sense of power filled her. This man wanted her. Badly. He was trying so hard to push her away.

"I'm not embarrassed," she said.

"I've had a lot of women throw themselves at me."

Brynn smiled. She reached out and pressed a palm to his chest.

He tensed.

"I can feel your heart racing," she murmured.

He stayed motionless. He was fighting so hard, but she knew it would be so good if he let go.

"God, you're handsome. Those dark, good looks. You have these sexy lips, so at odds with the rest of you. It gives me all kinds of ideas."

His gaze raked over her naked body, and she guessed he didn't know that violent hunger was churning in his eyes. In the end, he had to make the choice. She didn't want to take, she wanted him to meet her in the middle.

"You make me want, Vander. Everything."

His control broke.

She practically heard the snap as he surged up out of the chair.

His arm snaked around her and he lifted her off her feet so easily, making her realize just how strong he was.

Gasping, her nerves alive, Brynn wrapped her legs around his lean waist.

"There's no going back now," he growled. He slid a hand into her wet hair, tugging her head back.

Her pulse jumped.

"You're mine now, Brynn. I tried to warn you, but

you wouldn't listen." His mouth grazed her jaw. "*Mine*. I won't give you up. I won't let anyone take you from me. And I won't let you walk away."

Her belly clenched, heat flooding her at the possession in his voice.

"You'll give me everything I want. And after that, I'll take even more."

She met his turbulent gaze. "I'm yours. It's not taking, if I give it to you."

With a savage sound, his mouth crashed down on hers.

CHAPTER THIRTEEN

His blood was running hot. Vander needed this woman more than he needed to breathe.

More than anything.

He plundered her mouth. *Jesus. This.* This was what he needed. Her hot mouth. Her tight, sexy body.

Vander crossed the deck and laid her on a lounger. She was slick and damp—all naked beauty that he had to claim.

Her hand clamped on his head, her tongue stroking his. It was no surprise that Brynn kissed with every ounce of herself. She rubbed against him like she needed it as much as he did.

Like she was hurting as much as he was.

Fuck. He'd never wanted or needed anything as badly.

Vander stroked his hands down her body and she arched. He cupped her breast, thumbing her nipple. She moaned. He gently ran his fingers over the bruise on her ribs.

He looked up, at kiss-swollen lips and slumberous eyes. The bruising didn't take away from what he saw.

"Damn, you're beautiful, Brynn."

"*Vander.*"

The shining need in her eyes was like gasoline to the fire in his gut.

He shoved her thighs wider, and moved to his knees beside the lounger, then he ran his teeth down her thigh.

She shuddered. "*Wait.*"

"No," he growled. He took her in, all spread out for him. "Look at you." There was just a small strip of caramel-colored curls above a pretty, plump pussy. The desire in his gut raked him. She was like a damn light in the darkness.

Vander lowered his head. He dragged his tongue over her.

"Oh, God." She bucked. "Damn, of course you'd be good with your tongue."

Like a man possessed, he licked and sucked. He slid an arm around her hips and yanked her closer to his mouth. He wanted to find every sweet spot, every one of her secrets.

She went wild under his mouth.

"God, Vander—" The next few sounds were choked moans.

He worked two fingers into her tight, hot wetness. Damn, she'd strangle his cock. He couldn't wait to pump inside her. He found her clit, working it with his tongue.

"Yes." She writhed, wild sexy, with desperation and desire in her eyes. "I'm going to come. I'm going to—"

He pumped his fingers deep.

Her muscles bunched, her hips lifted. She cried out and he watched the orgasm take her. Satisfied pleasure filled him as he watched her face, and drank in every detail.

She dropped back, panting, her dazed gaze locked on him.

She reached up and tugged at his shirt. Buttons flew everywhere, and with a hungry sound, she reared up and bit his pec.

Fuck.

He shuddered. As her mouth moved over his skin, he shoved the ruined shirt off.

"Now," she whispered, her voice laced with desire.

"Now." He shoved her back and opened his pants. His cock sprang free, and her gaze locked on it.

He pushed her back, and dragged her to the edge of the lounger. Both of them were breathing hard and fast.

He dragged the head of his cock through her wet folds.

They both moaned.

"No condom," he bit out. He wanted nothing between them.

"No condom," she agreed.

He wouldn't ever get enough of her. He took her in—the strong face, flush with desire, those intelligent eyes, the sweet curve of her breasts, the dip at her waist, and those long legs he wanted wrapped around him.

Unable to hold back any longer, he thrust inside her. A savage possession.

Brynn cried out, gripping his arms, her nails digging deep.

A devastating ripple of pleasure moved down his spine. He stayed there for a quivering second, absorbing the tight, hot feel of her.

There it was. His everything.

A part of him had always known, from the moment he'd first seen her. It was why he'd fought so hard.

He pulled out, then plunged back in. His thrusts were hard and possessive, but he couldn't slow down. Gentle was beyond him right now.

But Brynn met every single thrust, choked sounds of pleasure coming from her.

His heart was a thundering roar in his ears, and he watched the place where his cock moved in and out of her sweet body.

Taking him every single time.

"God, Vander." Her nails scratched him harder.

He leaned down and kissed her. It was hard and hungry.

He felt the licks of hot pleasure growing, building into something huge. His hips moved faster, her cries growing as he pounded into her.

Everything was slipping, crumbling, falling apart.

He clenched his muscles.

She bit his lip. "Let go."

Those crystal eyes met his, stayed there.

On his next thrust, she screamed, hand fisting against his shoulder. He felt the orgasm rip through her, her pussy rippling on his cock.

With his next thrust, he stayed lodged deep in her.

He'd never surrendered before, but he did now. To her. To Brynn.

His body bucked as he jetted inside her. He groaned, then buried his face in her thick hair. His breathing was as labored as hers.

Shit. As his body cooled, he felt a lick of unfamiliar panic.

She was it for him.

She'd ruined a life of careful control. She could carve him up, bring him to his knees.

Vander had never, ever given anyone that kind of power over him.

He tried to pull back. He needed some space and time to reassess.

But she held him tighter and made a lazy sound.

"I knew it would be good," she murmured. "But that exceeded all expectations."

"Glad you approve." *There.* His voice was steady, even.

He felt her gaze on his face.

Something told him she saw too damn much.

She stroked a hand across his chest and he fought back the sensation.

"So, we didn't use protection," she said. "I'm on contraception."

"I know. Depo-Provera. You get the shot regularly. And you had a checkup three weeks ago, which included a STD check."

Her eyebrows went up. "Man, you PIs really dig deep in your investigations."

"I'm also clean. I wouldn't put you at risk, Brynn."

He couldn't stop himself. He stroked a thumb over her bottom lip. "I get regular tests, and I've always used condoms before."

That dark possessive need for her had consumed him. Made him do things that he'd never done before.

Fuck.

He pulled free and sat up. He needed to get a grip on this.

BRYNN STUDIED the bronze skin of Vander's back and her breath caught.

He had black ink on his back, centered on his spine. It was a warrior. The man looked vaguely Japanese, but it was hard to tell, as you could only see his back. He had thick, dark hair, no shirt, and his arms were raised, holding a sword.

A warrior on a warrior.

She reached out and touched it, felt him stiffen.

She was feeling too damn good to let him ruin this. She saw the way he was trying to hold back, and put space between them. A part of her worried that he didn't want her enough to fight past his own defenses.

She traced the black ink. "This suits you."

He glanced over his shoulder at her.

That dark-blue gaze drifted down her body, then came back to her lips.

Oh, he definitely wanted her.

He was just fighting it.

She smoothed her hand up his back and felt his small shudder, his muscles flexing.

Brynn stilled. She was a detective, used to reading between the lines, evaluating the evidence, and piecing the clues together.

Vander was a heavily controlled and contained man. She knew he didn't do relationships. No casual touches, no lazy caresses, or impromptu hugs.

She shifted in behind him.

"You hungry?" he asked.

"Hmm." She pressed her lips to his shoulder. She took her time kissing him, sampling his skin. She stroked her other hand up and down his strong spine, over that warrior's image.

She pressed up against his back, and nibbled on his ear. "I really, really like your body, Norcross."

"Yours is nice, too."

She bit his neck, heard him stifle a groan. She much preferred that to the even, cool tone.

Power filled her again. She affected this strong man. She could bring him pleasure or pain, hurt or comfort.

For a man with control issues... Yeah, she knew this was tough for him.

She was going to seduce him again. Only let him feel pleasure.

His hands gripped her thigh. "I just fucked you and came hard. I shouldn't want you again."

Brynn slithered around and straddled his lap. His hands gripped her hips, his fingers biting into her skin.

"You don't like it," she said. "Wanting so much."

"No."

She lifted her chin. "I'm not forcing you. You can get up and walk away at any time."

"No," he growled. "I can't."

Elation filled her. "I'm going to seduce you this time. You're going to lie back and take it."

His lips twitched and she loved that small movement.

She urged him back on the lounger. Her heart went a little crazy. The man was gorgeous, pure male perfection, and all hers for the taking.

She straddled his muscular thighs and slid her hands up his defined abs. He was all muscle. Built for strength and speed. And stamina.

He had more ink on one pec. She read the words. "Freedom is never free."

"So I never forget," he said.

She traced the letters.

He gripped her chin. "Say my name."

"Vander," she breathed.

He pulled her down for a deep, possessive kiss that left her trembling.

"Tell me how much you want me," he demanded.

She lifted up a little, caught by the dark glint in those eyes. A glint that warned her that he'd never let her go. Warmth filled her belly. She also saw the edge under it. A man not easy with needing someone so much.

She spread her hands over his pecs. "I've never wanted anyone the way I want you. I'll never want anyone like this again."

He growled. "Show me."

His cock was hard again, and she gripped the long thickness and stroked.

There was stark need on his face. She took her time exploring him. She planned to spend a lot more time here, but right now, she needed him inside her.

She lifted her hips and met Vander's gaze.

Brynn slowly lowered herself down, taking him inch by tantalizing inch. She moaned, feeling him stretch her. Feeling the slick heat of their union.

One. Nothing between them.

"Fuck. *Brynn.*" His hands cupped her ass.

God, the look on his handsome face. The need, the want, the dark possession. Her pussy clenched on him, and he bucked.

"God, you're tight," he grunted. "Ride me. Open those pretty thighs wider, and take me."

Brynn obeyed with a husky cry.

She planted her hands on his chest and rode him, working herself up and down on his cock.

His hands dug into her ass cheeks, urging her on.

She tried not to hurry or rush. She slid her hands down to his and pulled them off her. She entwined her fingers with his.

Their gazes met.

"Do you feel how much I want you, Vander?"

"Yeah." His low voice was guttural.

She kept moving her hips. "Any time I look at you, hear you talk, see you do something badass, I'm wet."

A growl vibrated through his chest. He jerked beneath her, filling her deeper.

"You said you won't give me up, or let anyone hurt

me, or let me walk away." She arched, taking him deeper, but she didn't lose his gaze. "Same goes, Vander Niccolo Norcross. I won't give you up, or let anyone hurt you, and I won't let you walk away, either." She felt the slow build of her orgasm growing, threatening to spill over her. She quickened her pace, their flesh slapping together.

"*Brynn.*" He said her name like a prayer.

She cried out, riding that pleasure-pain edge that only came before a blinding orgasm.

He thrust up, going deeper. "Get there, because I'm going to come inside my tight, sexy woman now."

She moaned.

"*Get there.*" His finger found her clit, rolled.

Brynn couldn't form any words, had no time. Her orgasm hit her hard, her body bowing and shaking. The pleasure was so huge.

Vander pumped up into her a final time and snarled. "Christ, Brynn." His fingers clenched on her.

His face contorted with pleasure, and even through her own release, she knew she'd never seen anything so sexy.

"*Mine,*" he murmured.

She slumped down, stroking his arms. She felt like she needed to comfort and reassure them both. "Yours. And you're mine." Jeez, neither of them could manage full sentences.

He stroked a hand down her back, and she kissed him lazily.

She stayed there, him still inside her, and enjoyed the simple pleasure of having her man connected to her.

His lips touched her neck, and finally, he gathered her limp body close.

"I'm hungry now," she mumbled.

She heard his low laugh. "I'm not surprised. I'm pretty sure you burned a few calories, Detective." He squeezed her ass. "Come on. Let's eat."

CHAPTER FOURTEEN

"I'm fine, Hunt. We're both fine."

Vander leaned back in his chair, listening to Brynn talk to Hunt.

She'd already spoken with her mom, her brother, and both her sisters. Vander had fielded messages from his own parents and siblings.

"Uh-huh." She took a swig of her beer, caught his gaze, and rolled her eyes.

They were back out by the pond again. Golden afternoon sunlight filtered through the trees. Brynn had found one of his T-shirts, and looked ridiculously appealing in it. He'd given her some oil and she'd removed the fake tattoos off her arm. Her bare legs were curled up on the lounger. He wondered what she had on under it.

He flexed the fingers of his right hand. There was nothing to stop him reaching under the cotton to find out.

He knew that she'd happily give him everything he demanded.

His cock throbbed. *Damn.*

He reached for the plate on the low table between them. They'd put together a platter with some cheese, crackers, dip, salami, grapes, and olives. He snagged an olive and sipped his own beer.

"Yes, yes, he's taking good care of me." Her gaze turned amused.

Troublemaker. They both knew Hunt would have a coronary if he knew exactly how Vander was taking care of her.

"Okay, keep me posted." She dropped her phone on the lounger and scrunched her nose. "So, Nomad has gone to ground. Hunt raided the clubhouse, but he was gone. No one is saying where he is."

"They're afraid of him."

She slumped back. "Yeah." Another pull of her beer. "Apparently Nomad is good at collecting information on people. Information they'd prefer to stay hidden."

"He had something on Trucker."

"Yes. Hunt says it's something to do with an old murder of a rival biker. From when Trucker was younger. That's all he knows. Hunt's informants are flooding him with info." A line creased her brow. "There are new drug shipments about to pour into San Francisco."

Nomad wasn't wasting any time. "That's what my informants are saying, too."

She sat up, her gaze sharpening. "Were you planning to tell me that?"

"Yes."

"When?"

God, that suspicious tone. He held up his phone.

"Ace just sent the intel through while you were on the phone."

"Oh."

"Not very trusting, are you, Detective?"

She extended one long leg and kicked his shin. "You're a bit of a shady character, Norcross."

He grunted, wondering again what she had under that shirt.

"We need to stop the shipments and find whatever rock Nomad has crawled under," she said.

"I have Ace working on it. We'll intercept the drug shipments, and we'll find Nomad." Vander wasn't letting that asshole get away with infiltrating his city and turning it into his own little drug playground.

Or attacking his woman.

His chest tightened, but he absorbed the emotion. How he felt about her.

"I'm not going to see one more kid's life cut short." Her light-blue eyes fired. "When kids are hurt or killed, it's the worst."

He saw the darkness in her eyes. That familiar darkness he saw in the mirror every day.

He reached out and took her hand. "Think of the ones you've saved."

She swallowed, and studied him. Yeah, he knew she'd see his own darkness.

Fuck, the things he'd seen. Done.

"These overdoses get me," she said quietly. "Kids on the cusp of adulthood, about to plunge into the prime of their lives. All that potential. But the worst was a few weeks back." She stroked a finger down the condensation on her bottle. "I was too late to stop an asshole stepfather from beating his toddler stepdaughter to death. He was sky-high on Stardust and out of his mind. Shit." She blew out a breath.

"I know." Vander did. That sense of helplessness. The sense of failure and despair that the world was fucked.

She nodded. "You're right. I need to focus on the good stuff. The kids I did help get out. The women I've saved. The men I've helped."

Yes, but Vander was aware it wasn't always that easy.

His gaze turned inward. He saw the face of every man he'd lost, every enemy he'd killed, every civilian he'd failed to save.

"Hey." Brynn slid onto his lap and cupped his cheek. "Stay here with me."

When he looked at her, she smiled. Smiled like he deserved it.

Light shone out of her. She might've seen the darkness, but she hadn't let it taint her.

She rose. "I feel like another swim."

She pulled the T-shirt over her head, and he finally got to see what was under it.

His cock went hard in an instant. It was a tiny bikini that Gia had probably left there. It was red, and very small. It had ties at the sides of the bottoms, and small triangles that barely covered Brynn's breasts.

She turned and dived neatly into the pond.

He watched her swim. Hell, he'd be happy watching her breathe.

"Come and join me," she called out.

Her hair was slicked back, and her smile was one he couldn't resist.

Damn. He couldn't lose every shred of his control around her. It was too dangerous.

He shook his head.

She swam closer, that smile still in place.

Then she splashed him.

Water soaked him. Vander stood, watching as she swam away, laughing.

He narrowed his gaze, then pulled his drenched shirt off. That got her attention.

And when he shucked his wet jeans and boxers, she stared.

He dove into the pond.

"Payback," he warned.

"It was just water," she said breathlessly.

As he sliced toward her, she took off. They chased each other across the pond. The sound of her laughter worked its way inside him. He caught her ankle, but she kicked free, quick and sleek.

"Come on, Norcross. You need to be faster than that."

She shot past him, her wet body brushing his. Then she splashed him again.

He smiled. *Game time was over.*

Vander lunged after her.

He caught her in two strokes. He circled her waist and yanked her back against him. He fitted her slim back to his front.

She gasped, laughing again. His hard cock rubbed against her ass, and her laughter turned to a choked sound.

"What are you going to do now?" he murmured in her ear, sliding a hand over her belly.

"Nothing." She turned her head to look at him. "I'm right where I want to be." Then she blinked, wonder on her face. "God, Vander. I love when you smile."

He realized he was smiling down at her.

Need hit him.

She was like a firefly, bright and pretty, but he wanted to catch her and keep her all to himself.

He spun her and hauled her up.

She eagerly wrapped her arms and legs around him.

Vander wasted no time. He shifted her and yanked her down, loosening the tie on the bikini bottoms. His throbbing cock thrust inside her with one smooth plunge.

He caught her startled cry with his mouth, and slid a hand into her wet hair. "Now I have you right where I want you."

He planted his feet and held her as she started to move on him. Water splashed around them.

"Hold on tight, Detective."

"I'm not letting you go, Vander."

Then he let her drive them both wild.

Reality would intrude soon enough, but right here, right now, she was all his.

BRYNN WOKE the next morning with a hard male body curled protectively around her.

Vander was a wall of heat at her back, with one arm snaked around her, a hand cupping her breast.

They'd slept like this all night. Vander kept her pinned close, his body shielding hers. Well, when they weren't having lots of hot sex. He'd woken her more than once.

God, this felt good.

Waking up, right here, tangled up with this man... Her heart did a little stutter.

Now, she just had to convince Vander that this was right.

She breathed in his scent. She didn't doubt he had feelings for her. It was dealing with those feelings and the vulnerability they brought that was his problem.

A man like Vander, who'd been honed to recognize and eliminate risks, wouldn't like having a weakness.

She needed him to trust that she would look after herself.

Slowly and carefully, she turned in his arms to take in his outrageously attractive face. He was too rugged to be classically handsome, but the man was far too hot for his own good. The dark stubble on his jaw made him look even more dangerous.

Lazy heat curled through her. She had stubble burn in a few delicate places, plus a few other interesting aches. Unsurprisingly, Vander Norcross had impressive stamina.

Brynn realized there would always be some risk in their world. They both had jobs that came with it. She needed to show him the other benefits. It didn't have to all be danger, bad guys, and stress.

Softly, she pressed her mouth to his chest. She peppered kisses over that bronze skin, then moved lower.

The man was all muscle, with zero percent body fat. She felt him stir, one hand sliding into her hair.

"Good morning." His voice was still gruff from sleep.

She looked up his body and smiled. "Morning. It's about to go from good to great."

That got her one of those rare smiles. "Really?"

She curled her fingers around his cock and stroked. "Really."

She slid lower, raking her teeth over his hipbone. *God, these abs.*

Vander shifted, pushing up on the pillows. His gaze locked on her.

Brynn stroked his rigid cock, then took him in her mouth.

His groan was low and deep.

She took her time. She didn't want to rush this. Right now, in this bed, at his cabin, they were in a safe, little cocoon. Reality was very far away.

But she was excruciatingly aware that it would intrude before she was ready.

She used her tongue and lips. She sucked him harder.

"Damn, Brynn." His body was tense beneath her. "*Christ.*"

He moved like he was going to sit up, and try and take over.

"No!" She slid her mouth off him, then pressed his hands to the bed. The man liked to be in control far too much. Especially in bed. He let her explore, but it almost always ended with him pinning her down until she came. He was good at it, so she had no complaints.

But this time, she was making *him* let go.

She tapped his wrists. "Keep them there."

His dark-blue eyes flashed, but he sank back on the pillows.

She felt a flush of satisfaction.

She lowered her head and once more sucked that beautiful cock back into her mouth.

"*Brynn.*"

His big body vibrated, but he didn't take over. He wrapped a hand around hers at the base of his hard cock. They worked him together, when she looked up at him, she saw fire, and so much more in those midnight eyes.

"I'm close," he groaned.

She picked up speed, sucking harder. His powerful body arched, his cock going deeper, then he came down her throat.

As he collapsed back on the bed, she licked him slowly, then worked her way back up his body.

It shocked her just how much she enjoyed pleasuring him. She lay flush against him, filled with satisfaction.

"It is a great morning," he said.

She smiled at him.

He yanked her close and kissed her hard.

"I'm going to bake cookies," Brynn announced.

He raised a dark brow. "For breakfast?"

She sat up. "Yeah. I don't get the urge often, but all these orgasms must have inspired me."

That got her another smile. Her heart squeezed.

Every one made her feel like she'd won a prize. "I saw

flour and sugar in the cupboard when I snooped earlier. What's your favorite cookie?" Her gaze dropped to his stomach. "Or do you not eat cookies?"

"Chocolate chip," he said.

"Chocolate chip it is."

After a quick shower, she found one of Vander's business shirts and rolled up the sleeves. She also found a pair of denim shorts that were just a tiny bit too tight, but still manageable.

She got to work in the kitchen. Vander sauntered in a short while later, wearing a pair of navy-blue cargo shorts, and a blue polo shirt.

"Any news from San Francisco?" she asked.

He shook his head. "Ace is working on it." He sat on a stool.

She poured him some coffee. Black with one sugar.

He looked at it. "You're good, Detective."

"I am."

She pulled out all the ingredients she needed for the cookies. He'd bought a block of chocolate, and she broke it into chunks.

He watched her as she mixed the dough.

"So, the Bruins beat the Sharks," he said.

"Bummer."

"That means I win our little wager."

She started rolling the dough into balls and flattening them on a tray. "It does. What do I owe you?"

He leaned forward. "Exotic sexual favors."

She grinned. "You drive a hard bargain, Norcross. Guess I'll have to pay up."

"I'll let you know." He watched her set more cookie dough out. "You like to bake?"

"Only when I feel inspired. I don't have much time to experiment in the kitchen. My mom taught me to bake. My sister, Naomi, is the best at it. My regular cooking is nothing to write home about, though."

"I can cook," he said.

Brynn froze. "Come again?"

His lips quirked. "I'm sure you know my mom is Italian-American. Well, she vowed that all her kids would be able to cook."

"You can cook Italian food?" Brynn breathed.

He smiled. "Yes. My specialty is pizza dough from scratch."

"That's it, we have to get married now."

His gaze went to hers, held.

Heart pounding, she fought hard to keep her face easy, casual. She winked, then turned to slide the tray of cookies into the oven.

She set a timer and then leaned on the messy island. "So, I've been thinking about a way to find Nomad."

Vander's face turned serious. "We'll find him eventually."

"But how many more people will get hurt? How many more kids will overdose?"

"Brynn—"

She shook her head. "I have an idea. We lure him out."

Vander watched her with that intensity of his.

"He's fixated on me," she said. "He thinks I'm a snitch."

Vander's brows drew together.

"He wants revenge. That's big with the Wanderers. So...you use me as bait to lure him out."

For a second, Vander was stock-still.

Then he shot to his feet. "*No.*"

CHAPTER FIFTEEN

Brynn steeled herself. "Vander, we—"

He shook his head violently. "Absolutely not."

She fought for control of her own anger. "I'm a cop. That's all I've ever wanted to be. I wanted to help people, like my dad did."

A muscle ticked in Vander's jaw.

"My dad loved being a cop. Kids drew him pictures, people baked him things to say thank you. I idolized him." She swallowed. "Every day, I try to live up to his memory and make him proud."

Vander was silent for a moment. "Tell me what happened to him?"

"You already know. I gave you the highlights, and it's in whatever report you put together on me." Her stomach churned.

"But I haven't heard you tell me."

She sucked in a breath. The pain was old, but it still hurt so much. "His partner started taking bribes. A little here and there. To pay the bills. For a college fund for his kids." She closed her eyes for a second. "A deal went bad, and my father caught him. Dad was shot. Three bullets to the chest. One minute he was there, so big and so alive, and the next he was gone."

"I know how that feels."

Yes, Vander had lost men he'd fought alongside. He knew that pain.

"I can't stand by and let bad people get away with doing bad things. My father didn't. I can't hide." She walked toward Vander. His body was stiff, his jaw like rock. "Not even to make you feel better."

"There has to be another way." His tone was razor sharp.

"I'll be the bait, but we'll plan it. Hunt, you, and me. We won't take unnecessary risks." She pressed her hands to his chest. "We can flush out Tony Garcia and take him down. It's worth whatever risk."

"Not to me."

His body was strung tight, and she saw how hard his jaw was. "Vander—"

He moved fast, one big hand circling her throat. She froze and he leaned in.

"Do you know what he'll do to you?"

"He's not going to get me."

Vander shook his head, terrible emotions churning in his eyes. "I know you've seen horrible things on the job, but in a war zone, you can't even imagine what people can do to one another, let alone their enemy."

"Don't go there," she whispered. "I'm right here, Vander."

He yanked her against him. "I want to keep you right here. Alive and breathing."

God. Her man. She wrapped her arms around him.

"I have to take Nomad down. This is my job. What I was born to do. If you try and lock me up, it'll kill me. I need you to stand beside me, Vander, not in front of me." She looked up at him, saw things working behind his eyes. "If I stood aside and played the damsel, you wouldn't feel the same way about me."

"You'd hate yourself," he said quietly. "*Fuck.*" He dragged in a breath. "I *hate* this. Dangling you like juicy bait."

"You don't think I can handle it?" Her belly clutched.

He pulled back, dark eyes glittering. "Oh, I know you can, but that doesn't mean I have to like it."

Warmth bloomed in her...and another emotion she wasn't quite ready to process.

His gaze traced her face, then he made a low sound. He pulled her in for a hard, fierce kiss.

Oh. *God.*

She clung to him. The kiss was like a storm that had swept in with no warning, swamping her, dragging her under. He started backing her up.

Brynn kissed him back, and the low, hungry sound he made vibrated through her.

It ignited deep, dark desires.

"I need you," he said.

"So have me."

His mouth was back on hers, his hands everywhere. He cupped her breasts, and she moaned into his mouth.

He spun her and she found herself bent over the dining table.

She sucked in a breath, and felt him jerking her shorts open.

Yes. *Yes.* Wild, edgy excitement tore through her. She clenched her thighs, her panties already damp.

Sensation washed over her—her breathing was fast, her skin felt hot. Vander's mouth was on her ear, neck. He bit her and she arched.

He finished yanking her shorts down and then shoved her shirt up. He palmed her bare ass, making a deep, tortured sound.

Then he grabbed her arms, pulling them behind her back. Her upper body was pressed to the table, her cheek to the wood.

He kept both her wrists in one hand at her lower back. She tested his hold, and his grip tightened. He wasn't letting go. She felt him unfastening his shorts.

Brynn sucked in a breath, biting her lip.

"Fuck. *Fuck.*" He freed his cock, then with one thrust was inside her.

"Oh...*Vander.*"

He pulled back and thrust again. Both Brynn's body and the table shook. With steady, heavy thrusts, he possessed her.

And she loved it.

She tilted her hips, trying to take more of him.

His thrusts were relentless, every plunge sending electric jolts of pleasure through her. She felt the pressure build. A glowing, hot ball in her belly.

He kept pumping, and her climax exploded—fast and furious.

As the pleasure drowned her, she cried out his name. She shook under him, her body clamping down on his cock.

He growled, and thrust deep, his body covering her. She listened to him groan through his own orgasm.

Then he released her hands and slumped on her. His lips touched her neck.

His chest was heaving. Still drunk on the last echoes of her release, she smiled. She was so damn happy she could wring so much out of this man.

Her man.

She let out a happy sigh.

"I'm sorry," he said.

"Don't be on my account."

"I was rough."

"I know. It was glorious."

That got a bark of surprised laughter out of him. He pulled out of her and she bit her lip. His hands stroked down her back.

"I never told you that I like your tattoo." He touched the curve of her right butt cheek.

"Thanks." She had a small heart with a blue line through it. A symbol of the job she loved. She was too boneless to move. "I'll just have a little nap here."

He spun her and scooped her up like she weighed nothing. She managed a startled squeak.

When he dropped onto the couch, then stretched out with her, she nuzzled into him.

"Feel better?" she asked.

He sighed. "We plan this op down to the last detail."

She nodded.

"If I think it's going south, you're out. Period."

She saw the fear in his eyes. He usually hid it so well, but she'd become something of an expert at reading Vander Norcross.

"Okay," she agreed.

She felt his body relax.

"And you owe me extra sexual favors now," he added.

She bit her lip to keep from smiling. "Deal."

"I really didn't mean to be so rough." He stroked her jaw.

"Yes, you did. And I liked it." She rubbed her nose against his. "I do need one thing though."

"What?"

"A cookie."

The oven dinged.

He shook his head. "You never do what I expect."

She grinned at him. "That's never going to change, Norcross, so get used to it. Now, cookies."

―――――――

SITTING AT THE TABLE, Vander glanced at the tablet, the laptop, and the notepads spread out before them.

Brynn had one foot up on her chair, chin resting on her knee as she chewed on the end of a pen.

Vander was experiencing a problem he'd never had before—trouble concentrating.

He kept picturing fucking Brynn on the table. It was

messing with his focus. All he could see was that bare ass, her sweet body taking his cock.

She made a sound and scribbled something on a notepad. "Ace's intel on Nomad is good. He was getting too pushy and problematic at his old club in Arizona."

"So his boss sent him off to cause trouble somewhere else." They picked the wrong fucking city.

She made another notation. "To lure him out, it needs to be somewhere contained. I need to go in alone, but have you guys, and some undercover cops close."

Vander had learned that even though she was fine with technology, Brynn loved to write things down.

He still hated this plan.

Dangling her as bait for Nomad went against everything inside him.

"You wear a tracker," he said.

She looked up. "I—"

"It's non-negotiable. Ace has some that are microscopic. No one will find it."

"I—"

"No arguing," he bit out.

She leaned over and slapped her hand over his mouth. "I was going to say that I'm fine with that."

He raised a brow and she shifted her hand.

"You're humoring me," he said.

"No, Vander, I'm doing something to make my man feel a little more at ease."

Damn, he felt like she could see right inside him. He didn't really like it. He'd avoided letting people read anything often pretty much his entire life.

"Your man?" he said.

She rose and slipped onto his lap. "Well, if I'm your woman, that makes you my man. Boyfriend sounds *way* too juvenile."

He'd never been anyone's boyfriend, even when he was younger. He slid a hand down her thigh.

She grinned. "Want me to beat my chest? Me Brynn, you Vander. You—"

He took that sassy mouth in a hard kiss. "You're a troublemaker."

She looked a little dazed and breathless. It was his new favorite pastime to leave the competent detective a little mussed up.

"Yes," she said. "But I'm all yours."

He felt those words hit his chest, dead center. "You are."

And now he needed to find a way to keep her safe. Especially when she'd run headlong into trouble without hesitation.

He gripped her chin and kissed her again. No hesitation. She melted into him, kissing him back. He slid a hand under her shirt—actually, his shirt.

Suddenly, a low, male chuckle followed by a strangled sound filled the room.

Vander whipped his head to the laptop on the table.

A laughing Ace, a highly amused Saxon, and a pissed-off Hunt were looking at them on a video call.

"Oops." Brynn kissed Vander again, then slid back into her chair.

"I see having a bounty on your head and being in hiding is really tough for you," Saxon said dryly.

Vander shot his friend the finger, then shifted his gaze to Hunt.

The detective's face was carved from stone as he glared.

Brynn leaned forward. "Please, you can't beat each other up across the computer." She pointed at her cousin. "And this is none of your business."

"We'll see." Hunt pinned Vander with a hard stare. "You were supposed to protect her."

"I am."

"You and I will have a conversation."

Vander nodded.

"No, you won't." Brynn's eyes fired.

"We will," Hunt growled.

Her gaze narrowed.

"It's a guy thing," Vander told her. "You don't have the right bits to understand."

She rolled her eyes. "No, I actually have a brain that I use."

Out of sight of the camera, he pinched her butt. Then he looked back at the computer. "I assume you have something for us."

"If you can manage to pull yourself away from the lovely detective," Ace said with an unrepentant grin.

Hunt swiveled to glare at Vander's tech guru.

"What have you got?" Vander asked.

"Drug delivery coming in tonight. A big one."

Brynn leaned forward. "Where?"

"There's a nightclub re-opening," Saxon said. "The Cathedral. It's been closed for a full renovation. It's a multi-floor affair. Think lots of lights and lots of bodies."

It sounded like hell to Vander. "And?"

"It's owned by two young guys. Brownlee and Lindsey. They scrounged up a bunch of private investors to fund it. Not all of those investors are upstanding citizens."

Vander's jaw tightened. "One of them might've made a deal. To allow one of their private investors to run drugs in the club."

Brynn tapped her fingers on the table, her brow creased. "It's the kind of place that attracts an upscale clientele, with a lot of ready cash. Ripe for the picking."

"So they're going to deliver tonight?" Vander said.

Saxon nodded.

"We can't let that product flood the club or get on the streets," Hunt said. "And there is a chance the delivery driver might know where Nomad is."

"We need a plan," Saxon said.

"I can get some undercover officers in," Hunt said.

"They need to blend well," Vander warned. "Nomad will be watching this drop like a hawk."

"Any idea how it will get delivered?" Brynn asked.

The three men shook their heads.

"Likely, it'll have to be by truck." Vander frowned. "And everything would already be packaged up for easy delivery."

Hell. If they botched this, Stardust went straight into the hands of young people, and no doubt eventually kids.

"All right," Vander said. "We need to seed the club with our people. Be on the lookout for anything. Hunt has the lead."

The detective nodded. "We want to stop the drugs,

arrest the delivery drivers, and then I can bring Brownlee and Lindsey in for questioning."

"Ace," Vander said. "Keep digging for any more info."

Brynn leaned closer to the screen. "I want to be there."

Vander frowned. "Nomad is looking for you."

"For us. I don't care. This is *my* case and I won't allow these drugs to get loose." She met his gaze. "I won't let Nomad force us to hide forever."

"It's too dangerous."

She smiled. "Not if we go undercover." She cocked her head. "Do you like playing dress-up, Norcross?"

He crossed his arms over his chest. "No."

"Don't worry. By the time I'm finished, no one will recognize us."

Ah, hell. If he tried to stop her, she'd find a way to go anyway.

And wherever Brynn was, he was staying close. Besides, he wanted in on this anyway.

"We were planning to come back anyway," she continued. "We have a plan to lure Nomad out of hiding."

Hunt frowned. "How?"

"Use me as bait."

"No!" Her cousin speared Vander with a look. "You agreed to this?"

"No. But have you tried to argue with her?"

Brynn lifted her chin. "As an adult woman, who happens to be a police detective in charge of this case, I make my own decisions." She gave a small smile. "And there were possibly sexual favors involved."

Ace and Saxon grinned, and Hunt made a pained sound.

"We'll meet you at the office," Vander said.

Hunt frowned. "The Wanderers will have people watching your office."

"I have a secondary entrance. They won't see us."

"You're sure?" Hunt said.

"I'm sure. See you in a few hours, and then we'll crash a nightclub opening."

CHAPTER SIXTEEN

Brynn sat in the passenger seat of the rugged Mercedes SUV as Vander drove them back into the city.

She was sorry to leave the cabin behind, but she made a vow that they'd be back. She could do with a little more downtime, and there was no doubt Vander could.

He'd never fully relax at a crowded resort, but quiet weekends away by the pond... Yes, she could handle that.

She glanced his way and let out a little sigh. She could watch the man drive all day. Although—she stared at his strong hands on the wheel—now that she knew what he could do with those hands, and what his body looked like naked, and just how good his stamina was, she could think of other things to do.

She was totally going to make this man fall so hard for her that he'd want each and every tangle and complication they could make together.

"Brynn, quit looking at me like that, or I'll have to pull over."

He was staring straight ahead, not even looking at her.

"Sorry," she said. "If we had more time, I'd totally take you up on the offer though."

His lips quirked. "There's not much room in here."

"No, but I'm bendy."

She saw his fingers flex on the wheel. He looked her way. He was wearing a pair of reflective sunglasses, which just made him look hotter.

"Unfortunately, I'll have to prove my bendiness later," she said. "When we don't have a drug shipment to intercept."

"Yes." That deep voice held that lethal edge she loved.

As they drove into the city, she felt a fine tension fill her body. There was a bounty on their heads. Every criminal asshole in the city would be looking for them, dreaming of a big payday.

Finally, they reached South Beach. Vander pulled up at an office building just down the block from the Norcross Security office. He touched something on the dash and the parking garage door slid open. He drove down into the underground parking.

Brynn looked at him and raised a brow.

"I rent an office in the building." He pulled into a reserved parking spot and cut the engine. "Come on." He shouldered a small backpack and climbed out.

She got out and followed him across the space. There were several parked cars and their footsteps echoed on the concrete floor. He strode straight past the elevators, and led her to a nondescript door marked with "Maintenance" on it. He tapped a code into the pin pad lock and it beeped.

After he opened the door, he waved her inside.

It was just a bare, empty corridor, with some pipes running overhead. He led her to another door and unlocked this one with a thick, sturdy key.

Inside, was just dark, impenetrable shadow.

"I hope you haven't decided to cash me in for the bounty, Norcross."

"I can think of better things to do with you, Detective." He pulled something out of his backpack, then clicked on a large, tough-looking flashlight. The powerful beam of light cut into the darkness.

Brynn saw a bare tunnel with a curved ceiling. Vander set off.

"What is this place?" she asked.

"Old sewer tunnel. San Francisco has lots of old tunnels from sewers to old World War II bunkers." The tunnel turned slightly. "Don't worry. This one is cut off from the active sewer system now."

They kept walking. The tunnel made a few more turns before he stopped at a sturdy metal door. He unlocked a padlock and pushed the door open with a rusty screech of metal.

They stepped out into another parking garage. This one filled with a row of sexy, black SUVs.

She spun to look at him. "You have a secret, underground tunnel into your office."

Vander turned the flashlight off. "Yes."

"You are one paranoid, secretive man."

"I'm a cautious, well-prepared man."

"Sure, you keep on believing that, Norcross."

They headed upstairs and found the Norcross team waiting for them, along with Hunt.

"Brynn." Her cousin hugged her, then shot a look at Vander that should kill instantly.

Vander just raised a brow.

Hunt gently touched the bruising on her face.

"It doesn't hurt." She'd topped up on painkillers before they'd left. "I'll have to use some heavy-duty makeup to hide it."

"Any problems getting into the city?" Saxon asked.

"No," Vander replied. "Let's plan this mission."

"I pulled up the schematics of the club," Ace said.

They all filed into his office.

"The Cathedral has four floors. Each one has a different vibe."

Brynn studied the slick publicity photos of the club. There were colored lights everywhere.

"Jesus," Vander said.

"Who wants to drink while being blinded?" Saxon asked.

"Young people," Brynn said dryly.

Vander's brow creased as he studied the images. "Deliveries come in on the lower level."

"Yes. I've already hacked the CCTV and I'm monitoring the dock." Ace leaned back. "A lot of food and booze came in."

Brynn nodded. "So, we focus our attention on the lower floor."

"It's too dangerous for you to go in," Hunt said.

She put a hand on one hip. "I've been undercover for

several years, Hunt. No one will know it's me." She flicked a glance at Vander. "And Vander can do the same, no doubt."

Hunt didn't look happy.

"Who are you bringing from the team?" she asked.

"Wilson and Patel."

"Good choices." She'd worked with them before.

"And Saxon, Rhys, and I will be in the crowd too," Vander said. "Ace will provide comms from here."

"It'll be too noisy for our earpieces," the tech man said. "So put your phones on vibrate."

Hunt looked at his feet and dragged in a deep breath.

"She'll be covered," Vander said.

Brynn sucked in an outraged breath. "*She* is a highly trained and experienced cop. She can cover herself." She poked Vander in the chest. "Remember our conversation? Beside, not in front."

His gaze locked on her lips. "I remember."

"Good." She felt a flush of pleasure but didn't show it.

Then he did something very un-Vander-like. He grabbed her and kissed her in front of everyone. It wasn't long, but it was firm.

Hunt growled.

Fighting off a very inappropriate wave of lust—not good, when surrounded by your hot guy's friends and employees, and your cousin who was almost a brother—she faced Hunt.

He was glaring at Vander.

"You and I need to talk," Hunt said.

She poked her cousin this time. "About the club job?"

"No."

"You are not talking about my sex life."

Hunt winced.

"If I want to have sex with every man in this room, it is none of your business."

Saxon's low laugh was very appealing. Ace and Rhys were grinning. Vander scowled and didn't look that thrilled.

"It's okay, Vander," she said. "I only want to do you."

Saxon lost it again and Rhys joined him. A vein was bulging in Hunt's temple.

"Now, shall we talk work?" she asked sweetly.

Hunt flicked a glance at Vander. "She's always been trouble."

"I've already worked that out." Vander gave a slow smile. "I like trouble."

Oh, God, she was turned on in front of her cousin.

She cleared her throat. "Did you bring my bag?"

Hunt nodded to the large duffel bag sitting by the wall.

"You packed everything I asked for?"

"Yes," his cousin said.

"Thanks. I'm going to get ready for the club."

"We'll finalize a few details here," Vander said. "Go on up."

Brynn hefted her bag and headed upstairs to Vander's loft. She needed to get her head in the game. She'd never had this problem before, but Vander sure was hard to stop thinking about.

She dumped her bag in the guest bathroom and unzipped it.

There was an internal pocket and she quickly opened it, and pulled out a picture of her and her dad. She was in the middle of her awkward teen years. She smiled, and felt an edge of bittersweet pain. God, she missed him.

"I hope you're proud of me, Dad." The last few years had been all work for her. Making detective had been her goal, and now it was proving she was a damn good one. She rarely took time to be still, or just breathe.

She thought about swimming in the pond with Vander. Making love by the water. She'd relaxed then.

"You'd like him, Dad. Oh, you'd be pissed he was touching your baby girl, but I'm touching him back. I'm all grown up now."

She hoped wherever he was, he was watching. Well, not the sex bits. *Ew.*

Brynn slipped the picture away. Okay, time to transform.

She'd learned plenty of tricks while working under-cover. Keep it simple. It was more about body language and posture, than what you actually wore. People tended to see what they wanted to see.

She shimmied into a very short, very sparkly dress in a color that wasn't sure if it wanted to be blue or gray or pewter silver. She fidgeted until the girls were settled in the very low, plunging neckline.

"Please don't fall out," she whispered as she used a bit of tape.

She pulled her wig out and settled it into place. Then, she did her makeup. She used a lot of gunk to cover her bruising, then went heavy-handed with the eyeshadow and liner. Bright-red lips finished the look.

She slid some long, dangly, silver earrings into her ears—they almost brushed her shoulders. Then she sat on the toilet seat and fastened the straps of her sexy high heels. They were black, with shiny silver around her ankles.

She wished she could avoid the heels, but at a fancy club opening, that wasn't happening. She straightened and pulled a face in the mirror.

Her mother would walk past her without knowing her. *Right*. Time to get this show on the road.

She opened the door.

Vander stood in the living room, fastening the cuff of his navy-blue shirt that had a bit of shimmer through it. It was tucked into fitted gray pants. Very trendy, and very *not* Vander. Oh, he dressed well, but he was usually much more classic than this.

He turned, spotted her and he went still.

God. He'd styled his hair, and...put something in it to lighten it. The strands were tipped with gold.

And he was wearing dark-framed glasses, a leather necklace that looked great against his bronze skin, and a heavy black ring on one hand.

Her insides spasmed. *Mini orgasm*.

He didn't look like Vander Norcross. He looked like a rich, European playboy, back from a month sunning himself in the south of France.

Vander scowled. "What the hell are you wearing?"

"A dress. A dress a young woman going to a hot night-club would wear."

"You armed?"

She smiled and lifted the heel of her stiletto to show the long spike. Then she opened the small, sparkly bag on her shoulder to show her SIG. She'd wedged it into the bag.

"You look ridiculously hot," she told him.

"You look ridiculously fuckable."

That gave her a sweet shot of heat through the belly. "Then let's get this done and come back here. I'm looking forward to seeing your bed."

VANDER COULDN'T SEEM to find his usual sense of calm before this mission. He parked the X6 several blocks from the Cathedral club.

Brynn was already climbing out.

He circled the vehicle, his gaze running over her.

Hell, he was half hard, and had been since she'd walked out in that tiny, sparkly dress. It was gray-blue and covered in silver shimmer. It had long sleeves, but that was the only thing remotely demure about it. Its plunging neckline showcased her spectacular breasts, and the hemline was so short he hoped she didn't bend over.

She cocked her head, smiling with those red, red lips. She wore a wig—a sleek, black bob with bangs. Her eyes were smudged with dark color, her cheekbones looked sharp. She looked like a beautiful party girl out for a big night.

It wasn't just the outfit, or lack of it. It was the way she held herself. Shifting on her heels, smiling, flicking at her earrings and cocking her hip. An impatient woman with energy to burn on the dance floor.

She looked nothing like sensible, dedicated Detective Brynn Sullivan.

Damn, she was good.

"I much prefer the lethal, ex-military, badass-in-a-suit look, but your European playboy thing has some merit." She pressed a hand to his chest.

He raised a brow.

She leaned closer. "The glasses are *hot*."

Vander kissed her and then took her hand. They walked down the street.

There was a long line to get into the club, and lights strobed. He heard the faint throb of music from inside. It was Saturday night and people were out to party.

"We head in, split up, and look around." She leaned her shoulder against him like she was whispering sweet nothings. "If you see Hunt, pretend you don't know him."

"I'm good at sneaking around," Vander murmured. Albeit, usually in darkness, with a gun in his hand.

He slid the bouncer at the door a hundred so they could skip the lineup. The asshole was too busy eyeing Brynn's cleavage to say much.

Then they were inside.

It was as bad as he'd imagined. Garish lights blinked and strobed. The place was packed with gyrating bodies, and the music was a deafening throb.

"Come on." Brynn yanked him forward.

They waded into the crush, heading toward the long, sleek, black bar. It had lights running along it, and they changed colors with the beat of the music. He saw Brynn scanning both the staff and guests.

She leaned in and he smelled her. Her perfume

tickled the edge of his senses. She shifted and rubbed against him. Damn, she dissolved his control.

"We'll split up," she said. "I'll peruse the dance floor. You check out the tables and seating areas."

He squeezed her hip, and pressed his lips to her ear. "Be careful. No heroics, Detective."

She winked at him, then spun. He watched the sway of her hips in that tiny dress until the crowd swallowed her.

Vander did a walk-through. There were plenty of people drinking at the sleek, backless chairs and tables. A few people were undoubtedly high, but he saw no signs of drugs.

He did spot Saxon. The man was leaning against a high table, wearing a bright red shirt. Vander leaned on the other side of the table.

"Rhys and I cleared the upper floors," Saxon said.

Vander's gut said that the shipment was coming from the bottom level, but they had to rule everything out.

"Keep watch." He scanned for Brynn. He spotted Hunt in the crowd. The man was more dressed up than usual, and he didn't scream "cop", but unlike Brynn, he didn't quite transform into partygoer.

Vander kept looking around. One of the other undercover cops sat at the bar.

"Rhys slipped into the kitchen," Saxon said. "He should be back soon."

Vander lifted his chin. Where the hell had Brynn gone?

"Well, your woman's got some moves," Saxon said.

Vander followed his best friend's gaze, and his gut

cramped. Under a spotlight in the center of the packed dancefloor, he saw her. The lights flickered and changed colors with the beat of the music and caught the sparkles of her dress.

Her sky-high heels only made her toned legs seem even longer. She had her arms in the air, moving to the beat, and that brought several more inches of sleek thigh into view. She was seriously risking showing everyone her underwear.

And he wasn't the only one who had noticed.

Men, and a couple of women, watched her like circling sharks.

Lust coiled, hot and turbulent in Vander's gut. A guy with platinum-blond hair and white, white teeth moved in, sidling in behind Brynn.

Fuck, no.

Vander pushed off the table and heard Saxon laugh.

As he stalked forward, the crowd parted for him. One look at his face and people hustled out of his way.

The blond man tried to touch Brynn, but she whipped around and shoved him. The guy lifted his head, and that's when he spotted Vander. He froze like a very small animal sensing a predator entering the room.

Before Vander had even reached for the guy, Brynn stepped forward. She leaned against Vander, much taller in her heels, and bit his earlobe.

"Don't make a scene," she warned.

He slid his hands down her body. "You shouldn't have worn this dress."

She slid against him, moving to the beat of the music...and totally ignored his comment.

"Have you seen anything?" she asked.

"No." He nipped her jaw, then her lips. "You drive me crazy."

"Good. I think you need some of that in your life."

He spun her, so her back was pressed to his front. He didn't dance. Ever. But he moved against her. His fingers played with the hem of her tiny dress and stroked her skin. He saw her lips part and she rubbed her ass against him. *Minx.*

He squeezed her thigh. "If you make me hard right now, then there will be payback."

Her lips curled and she didn't look concerned.

His phone vibrated and he pulled it out. He sensed her playful tease sharpen to alertness.

"It's Ace." Vander tilted the screen so she could read it. *Delivery truck bringing drinks in now.*

"Let's check it out," she said.

Vander spotted Rhys by the dancefloor as they headed toward the kitchen.

"Hey!" Brynn threw her arms around Vander's brother like he was a long-lost friend. "Long time, no see."

Rhys patted her back, smiling. He glanced at Vander and raised an eyebrow.

They knew each other well enough to communicate without words.

You let her out in that dress?

Vander shrugged. *I didn't want to.*

Rhys' grin widened.

Vander curled an arm around her waist. "Drink delivery truck just arrived."

"Yeah, the staff mentioned that," his brother said. "Head honcho, Brownlee, one of the club owners, came down to check it was here. He was sweating and twitchy. The kitchen staff says he never comes down."

Brynn bounced on her heels. "This is it."

Vander jerked his head. "Let's move."

The three of them moved into the back hallway. Ahead, they saw two guys moving down the corridor carrying crates.

"Let me." Brynn sauntered forward. "New drinks!" she cooed.

"Who are you?" A tall guy with a bald head scowled at her.

"Sabrina. I work the main floor." Brynn fluffed her hair. "I'm parched. Let me—" She reached for a bottle.

The big guy slapped her hand away. "These aren't for you."

That was enough confirmation for Vander. He turned the corner and headed in their direction, Rhys behind him.

"Set the crates down, boys." Brynn straightened.

"Piss off, bimbo," the big guy said.

"Bimbo?" Brynn, whirled and punched the asshole in the gut.

It had to hurt, because he doubled over with a groan. The second guy froze.

The big guy stiffened, his face twisting. Vander sped up; the guy was a foot taller than Brynn.

But she swiveled, and kneed the guy between the legs. He made a wince-inducing sound.

Vander reached them, just as she rammed her heel into the guy's leg. The big guy crumpled.

"And it's Detective Bimbo to you," she drawled.

"Bro, I know she's yours, but I'm a little turned on right now," Rhys said.

Vander shot his brother a look.

Brynn crouched, and Vander hoped her dress covered everything important. She took a bottle from the crate and held it up.

Floating in the liquid was a little plastic baggy filled with clear, crystal-like chunks.

"Who's in charge of the delivery?" Vander asked.

The skinny second guy was frozen in fear. The big guy, still on the ground, spat out a curse.

Brynn lifted her heel again.

"Matias, he's in the truck," the small guy squeaked.

Just then, Hunt and his undercover officers burst into the hall. Saxon sauntered in after them.

"We're heading to intercept the guy in charge at the truck," Vander told them. "You got these guys?"

Hunt nodded.

"Product is in the bottles," Brynn said.

She took off down the hall, jogging toward the loading dock.

When they stepped outside, Vander saw a guy leaning against the truck, smoking. When he spotted them, he tossed his cigarette butt, spun, and started to run.

Vander leaped off the dock. He slammed into the guy, grabbed him, and jerked him around. Vander rammed the man against the truck.

"Hey, what do you—?"

Vander punched him in the face, cutting off the splutters. "Where's Nomad, Matias?"

The man's gaze narrowed. "You're Norcross." His gaze shifted to Brynn. "And you must be the police detective that Nomad is raging about." Matias grinned. There was blood on his teeth. "He wants you dead, Detective. And he wants to hurt you, first."

Vander shoved the man, slamming his head back against the truck.

"He's not afraid of you, Norcross."

"Then he isn't very smart. Where is he?"

"Don't know." The man glared at Vander belligerently.

"We'll see." Vander shoved the man at Rhys. "Put him in one of our holding cells."

Rhys glanced at Brynn.

She studied Vander's face, then nodded. "Take him. I'll run interference with Hunt."

"You walking into the gray, Detective?" Vander asked.

"No, I'm trusting you to help me get the job done."

CHAPTER SEVENTEEN

Brynn was mad and tired. A combination she hated.

On the good side, they'd stopped the drug shipment getting loose.

That was all the good she had.

She was sitting in the passenger seat of Hunt's Charger. After the nightclub fiasco, she'd gone to the station with a very-freaked-out David Brownlee, the club co-owner.

Vander had gone back to the Norcross office with a very militant Matias.

She hadn't heard from him, so she assumed that Matias was keeping his mouth shut.

Brownlee hadn't known anything worthwhile. She rubbed her face. He'd cried as she and Hunt questioned him.

He'd borrowed a lot of money for the nightclub renovation. He brought in many new investors, and made many promises, including giving what he thought were a few 'harmless' favors.

Like allowing one drug dealer investor to let a little product into the club.

Asshole.

She pulled off her wig. She'd already ditched her high heels. She scratched her itchy scalp, then readjusted her real hair in a ponytail.

She was still in her dress. Nothing said "serious cop" more than showing your boobs off to everyone you worked with. She mentally rolled her eyes. Whatever.

Hunt pulled into the Norcross office parking level.

"Maybe Vander had better luck with the driver," she said.

Hunt turned off the vehicle and rested his forearms on the steering wheel. "We should've taken Matias into custody."

"We'll get our turn." Brownlee hadn't known who Nomad was, let alone where he was. His investor was the middleman. A client of the Iron Wanderers.

"Brynn." Hunt grabbed her hand, his green eyes serious. "Vander...he's..." Hunt blew out a breath.

She pressed her hand over his. "I know exactly what Vander is." She saw elements of Vander in Hunt. When you fought for your country, you gave up a little piece of your soul. Yes, for a good cause, to protect, but it was still gone.

These tough heroes came back and had to learn to live without it.

Camden would be home soon. He'd be the same. She knew Hunt was worried about his youngest brother.

"Vander isn't an easy, or uncomplicated man," Hunt said.

She smiled. "I know. And neither are you."

"But I'm not like him. I... I always wanted a nice guy to give you a picket fence."

Brynn wrinkled her nose. "You think I want a picket fence?"

Her cousin scowled. "I'm speaking metaphorically here."

"Is it white? With a garden and a cute dog?"

Her cousin growled.

"Hunt." She cupped his cheek. "Vander can give me exactly what I want, what I need."

"You sure?"

"Yes. I'm falling in love with him."

"Shit."

She patted his scruff-covered cheek. "It'll be fine. Now go home and get some sleep. I'll see what Vander and the guys got from Matias. I'll message you if they got anything good."

"Tell Vander I'm coming tomorrow to arrest Matias, whether he likes it or not." His tone was still grumpy.

"Will do." She kissed his cheek. "Love you, Hunt."

"Go. You're such a pain in my ass."

Smiling, she slid out of the SUV. Damn, she needed a shower, Vander, and sleep. And she wasn't fussy about the order.

She saw Rhys waiting for her. The youngest Norcross brother looked tired, and his rockstar smile was missing.

"Hey," she said.

"Glad you're here." He took her arm and she felt a shiver of alarm.

"What's wrong?"

"Matias won't talk. The guy's clammed up tighter than a... You get the picture. Vander's not happy."

He led her through a doorway.

The holding cells were simple rooms with bare, concrete walls, a table, and a couple of chairs. There were three of them. Saxon stood with his arms crossed, looking through a glass window into one room.

Matias was handcuffed to a table. His face was bruised, but he was breathing. Vander was standing in front of him, one fist to the table. She looked at his face and shivered.

Oh, boy.

"Vander's been at it the entire time." Rhys shook his head. "He won't give up, and I'm worried he'll snap."

Saxon flicked a glance her way, his face grim.

"He won't." But she could tell Vander was riding the edge.

This one was pushing his buttons. She handed Rhys her wig and shoes, then strode into the room.

Vander's gaze landed on her like a heat-seeking missile. She suppressed a shiver. His eyes were dark, cold, turbulent.

She stroked a hand down his arm, then looked at Matias.

The man looked tired, his face pale, but he had a glint in his eye.

"Ah, the detective that Nomad wants to fuck up," the man said.

Vander stiffened.

"Ah, the idiot who doesn't know what's good for

him." She circled the desk, leaned in and lowered her voice. "Your boss might not think he should be afraid of Vander, but look at him."

She saw Matias lift his head, and she did the same.

Vander's powerful body was still tense. He was ready to attack. His gaze looked black, and she met it head-on.

She saw the ice-cold ruthlessness. And she also saw the hidden emotions.

For her.

Her belly coiled.

"He'll kill for me," she whispered. "He'll do anything for me."

Matias swallowed. "You're a cop."

She laughed. "You think that's going to save you?" She straightened, then strode to Vander.

She lowered her voice to a private murmur. "Let him stew a bit." She recognized the ones she needed to leave alone, in silence, with their own inner voices, before they'd crack.

Vander's gaze shifted back to Matias, hard and lethal.

She pressed a hand to his chest. "I need to get to bed before I fall down."

One more sharp look at Matias, then Vander took her arm and led her out.

"Leave him in there," Vander said to his brother and Saxon. "And get some rest."

"He needs time to stew." She yawned. "We stopped the drugs. Let's see what Matias says after a night chained to a desk. Is that chair uncomfortable?"

Rhys grinned. "Very."

"Good. Rhys, you play good cop. Leave him a bottle of water."

Saxon cracked a smile. "So he'll be stiff, sore, and have a full bladder in the morning."

She winked, then staggered into Vander a little. It wasn't entirely put on. She was dead tired, and her feet were aching.

"Come on." He wrapped an arm around her. "Bed."

She nodded meekly.

She saw Saxon's eyes widen a little as he realized her ploy.

She just smiled.

Vander led them into his apartment. Inside, she relaxed a little. "I need a shower."

He towed her into his bedroom.

Ah. It was a spacious room with lovely wood floors and a huge skylight overhead, above the big bed. There was lots of wood, and it was very Vander.

"Go, shower," he said. "I'll make us a snack."

"I'm too tired to eat."

"I know, but you need something. You didn't eat dinner."

He was looking after her. The man really was a mother hen. Looking after all his little chicks. She bit her lip. If she told him that, she'd get a killer scowl.

She wandered into the bathroom. It was as gorgeous as the rest of the space. She found her duffel bag had been moved in here.

Despite the wet dream of a long, hot shower, she bathed quickly and washed her hair. She pulled on fresh panties, but nabbed one of Vander's T-shirts to sleep in.

When she walked out, he was sitting on the bed. A plate of food rested on the bedside table, but all her attention was for him. He was so tense.

She sat beside him. "What's wrong?"

"Fucking Matias won't talk. I like better results than this."

"We'll see what morning brings. You know patience is needed in interrogations."

He shifted a broad shoulder. "Nomad wants to hurt you."

Ah, the real problem. "Nomad's not a nice guy. We already knew that."

"If he gets to you... If he touches you or hurts you..."

His real fear was rearing its head.

He was afraid she'd get hurt.

"That's not going to happen. You won't let it. And I won't let it."

Right now, her man needed a little extra care. How often did he come home and brood alone? Was no one ever here to help him relax?

She shifted behind him. "Shut it off now."

"It's not that easy."

She started massaging his shoulders. His muscles were all knots.

"I'll help you." She pressed a kiss to the side of his neck.

VANDER DROPPED his head forward as Brynn dug her fingers into his tight neck.

He'd never liked people touching him much, even as a kid. But he realized that he'd stay there like this all night, letting her touch him, if she wanted to.

What he felt for her had come too far, too fast. Grown so big.

"Relax," she whispered.

She pressed against his back, kneading his shoulders.

He usually relaxed with a glass of bourbon, alone.

Matias had spent hours taunting him, with everything Nomad would do to Brynn.

Usually, Vander didn't let assholes get to him.

But this time...

She hit a tight spot and he let out a small groan. She smelled of clean skin, his soap, and Brynn. Everything about her wound around him, seeped inside him.

Her fingers moved to his hair, rubbing his scalp.

"We'll recharge the batteries, then tomorrow we'll throw everything we've got at Nomad," she said quietly. "He's going down, no matter how often he and his goons run off their mouths."

Vander reached back and gripped her thigh. "Brynn... Don't get hurt."

She kissed his neck again. "That's not the plan. I need you to trust me. I've got this." She bit his ear. "I'm nasty when cornered."

She climbed onto his lap and kissed him. It wasn't fast and furious; this kiss was slow and drugging. A seduction.

She slowly unbuttoned his shirt and pulled it off.

"Lie down," she ordered huskily. "And lose the rest of your clothes."

As she moved onto the bed, he unfastened his pants and pushed them down with his boxers.

When he lay back on the bed, she turned off the lamp.

Silvery moonlight filtered through the windows and skylight. He watched her ditch her shirt.

His gaze stayed on the long, strong lines of her. She was no pushover. No one's target or victim.

She put a knee on the bed, crawling toward him, her damp hair spilling around her shoulders.

Temptress. A siren come to lure him to things he'd always wanted deep down, but denied himself.

She straddled him, then leaned down to kiss him.

There was still no rush, despite the heat building in a slow, fiery simmer.

Brynn bit his bottom lip, then stroked his chest. She moved lower and licked his nipple.

Fuck. He arched up. Such a simple caress, but he felt it deep. It was the emotion behind it, not the touch itself.

She shifted her hips and cupped his cock. She gave him a few lazy strokes, then she moved her hips, and slid him deep inside her.

"*Vander*," she murmured.

She rose and fell, taking him deep, joining them.

He watched in the silvery light that made her seem like a dream. She reached out and grabbed his hands, their fingers entwining.

Her hips moved faster.

"Do you feel it?" she panted.

"Yes." He bucked his hips up. "You're mine, Brynn. Always."

"Yes. *Yes.*"

He surged up and kissed her. She worked her hips faster, and a second later, the tension burst.

She cried out as her climax hit. Vander groaned and reared up. He shoved her onto her back and plunged inside her. He poured himself inside her to the sounds of her sweet cries.

Afterward, he collapsed against her.

He settled back on the bed, keeping her close. He pulled the sheet over them, and realized that she was already asleep, her hand resting over his heart.

Dammit, he hadn't gotten the chance to feed her. He stroked her hair. *Later.*

Vander looked at the shadowed ceiling and felt...calm.

So much of his life was noise, energy, action. He wasn't often still, and things were never really quiet.

But right here, with Brynn in his arms, her breath on his chest, everything was still and quiet.

"I'll protect you," he murmured against her hair. "I'll do whatever it takes to keep you safe, make you smile, give you what you need."

In her sleep, she nuzzled into him. Vander tightened his hold on her, then drifted off to sleep.

WHEN VANDER WOKE, the sun was shining through the skylight.

They'd slept later than usual, thanks to the late night. Brynn was mostly on top of him. He shifted out from under her and she snuggled into the pillow. He smiled. After their slow, magical loving, he'd woken her later in the night again for hard and fast. He was pretty sure he had some scratches on his back.

He rose, then just sat there, watching as she slept.

Finally, he dragged his gaze away. Her sparkly dress and shoes were on the floor. Her little sparkly bag was on the dresser and he noted her SIG spilling out of it.

He pulled on a pair of black trousers that he wore around home when he was alone, and didn't bother with a shirt. He got his gun cleaning kit, and then cleaned her weapon as he watched her sleep. Finally, he locked it in the gun safe.

She still hadn't moved, and he decided to make some coffee.

The coffee machine was humming when he heard the front door to his place open. Since everyone he knew was well aware that they'd had a late night, he knew instantly who it was. He spun and saw his parents walk in.

His former firefighter father was still tall and strong, despite his gray hair. His mother was shorter, curvy, and kept her curls colored dark.

His mother's gaze locked on him, and she made a beeline for him.

"A few messages saying you're okay, Vander Niccolo, is not enough."

"She needed to see with her own eyes," his dad added.

"Rome won't let us go anywhere without him." Clara Norcross threw her hands in the air. "I love that boy, but he wouldn't tell me anything. It took a lot of arguing to get him to bring us here."

Rome was well over six feet tall and packed with muscle. Vander wondered if anyone else called Rome a boy. Doubtful. "He's there to protect you."

"Because you're in danger." Her voice wavered.

"I'm all in one piece, Ma."

His mom threw her arms around him and hugged him tight. Vander hugged her back.

"You should put a shirt on. You'll catch a chill."

Vander grinned. His ma never changed. Never stopped fussing over her kids, no matter how old they were.

She looked up at him and cocked her head. "You look...different? More relaxed than usual."

She stared at him like a scientist with a specimen under the microscope.

"Even as a toddler you were never relaxed. Always watching and planning."

"I'm fine."

She touched his back, then frowned. "You're scratched up. You said you were okay."

Shit. He cleared his throat. "It's nothing."

Vander watched his dad's eyebrows wing upward, followed by a smile. Clearly, his dad had clued in.

"You want coffee?" Vander tried distraction.

His mother straightened. "Yes, I'll—"

"Norcross." Brynn's voice. She breezed out of the bedroom wrapped in a sheet. "Where's my SIG? It was on the dresser."

Ah, hell. Here we go.

"I cleaned it," he said. "While you were sleeping. It's in my gun safe."

She froze, her gaze on his speechless parents. Color filled her cheeks, but she rallied quickly.

She hitched the sheet up and painted on a smile. "You must be Vander's parents. I can see the resemblance." She came forward like she was wearing a ballgown, not a sheet. "I'm Brynn. Detective Brynn Sullivan."

His father's face changed. "You're a cop?"

Brynn nodded and shook his hand. "I've heard all about you, Mr. Norcross. My brother is with the fire department."

"Firefighter?"

She nodded. "He broke the family tradition of joining the police. We regularly give him hell about it."

Then Vander's mother took Brynn's hand and didn't let go.

"Brynn," his mother breathed. "Such a pretty name."

"Thank you."

Tears welled in his mother's eyes, and her gaze moved between them. Vander slid an arm around Brynn and his mother bit her lip.

"Ma, don't make a scene," he said.

She straightened, waved a hand, and dragged in a breath.

Vander's dad pressed a hand to his wife's back. "Now, now, Clara. Keep it together."

She shot her husband a look, then smiled at Brynn. "We'll take you both out for breakfast."

"That would be great, Ma, but we can't. I'm helping

Brynn with a case. We have to work." He wouldn't mention the danger from a gang of bikers.

"Ah." Disappointment slid onto her face. "Well, when you wrap your case up, you bring Brynn over for dinner. I'll make my lasagna."

Brynn smiled. "I love lasagna."

"We'd better get to work," Vander said.

"Oh, okay." His mom hugged him, hard. "Put a shirt on. And clean those scratches."

Brynn swiveled to look at his back and blushed.

He smiled at her.

Then he heard his mother's happy sigh.

As his parents walked out, he heard his mother's quiet sob.

"Hush now, darling," his dad said.

"They're cute," Brynn said before she winced. "Sorry about meeting them in a sheet."

"You worked the sheet." He paused. "Sorry about Ma crying. She..."

Brynn's lips quirked. "I know why she was crying, Norcross. You don't let women invade your space. You're crazy about me, and now she knows."

"I might need to step onto the terrace, since that healthy ego of yours takes up so much space."

She skimmed her hands up his chest. "You're totally tangled up in me."

He gripped her chin. That smile. "Cockiness and gloating are not attractive traits, Detective."

She opened her mouth to reply, but just then her cell phone rang.

"That's mine." She swirled in a cloud of cotton fabric.

"Hunt? Okay, hang on." She put it on speaker, her face serious.

"There's been a huge Stardust overdose at an apartment building near the University of San Francisco," Hunt said.

Brynn cursed. "No."

"Two are dead, and the others are on the way to the hospital."

"Fuck," she bit out.

"We caught it early. An anonymous caller called it in. The paramedics got to the victims fast."

Vander stiffened. "It's a trap."

Brynn nodded. "They're hoping I turn up."

"Someone probably saw you at the club," Vander said. "Reported to Nomad."

She nodded. "This is our chance to find Nomad and end this."

Vander's gut hardened. That once-unfamiliar fear was starting to feel horribly familiar. It was like a ball of lead in his gut. "Yes."

Now, he had to find a way to send her into the lion's den, but keep her breathing.

CHAPTER EIGHTEEN

Brynn rubbed the itchy spot on the back of her neck. "Quit touching it."

She glanced at Vander in the driver's seat of the X6. Unsurprisingly, he was tense and radiating menace.

He gave her the impression that he wanted to rip someone's head off. She started to scratch again, then dropped her hand to her lap. It was the location where Ace had stuck the small transparent tracking device on her. She was back in her usual work gear—jeans, shirt tucked in, gun and badge.

"I'll go in and assess the scene—" she thought of the dead young people and it made anger and sorrow cramp her gut "—and parade around enough for Nomad to see me."

A muscle ticked in Vander's jaw.

She reached over and gripped his thigh. "Hunt and the cops are in the building. You, Rhys, and Saxon will be just around the corner."

He lifted his chin.

"It's going to be fine. On the very slim chance Nomad gets me, I have the tracker."

"Think I'll just leave it on you even after this is all over."

Her heart squeezed. Did he realize he was talking like he wanted something long-term?

He pulled to a stop in front of the apartment building. The area was popular with students at the university. She saw the uniformed cop standing at the front door.

"I'll be around the corner," Vander said.

"I know." She leaned over and kissed him.

She'd been planning to keep it brief, but he gripped her chin and deepened the kiss, his tongue plunging deep.

Need pulsed inside her.

God, would it always be like this? One look, one touch, one taste, and desire would just explode inside her.

But under that desire was a sense of rightness. Like coming home.

She nibbled his lip. "Let's do this, arrest Nomad, and go home."

Dark-blue eyes studied her.

"And then I want you to take some time off," she added. "I want to go back to the cabin and lie by the pond."

Warmth bloomed in the chill of his eyes. "You do owe me many and varied sexual favors."

She rolled her eyes.

"Go get your man, Detective."

"Oh, I've already got him." She cupped Vander's jaw. "But I'll go get the bad guy."

She opened the door and got out. As she walked toward the uniform, the X6 stayed where it was parked. She rolled her eyes again. She knew that Vander wouldn't move until she was safely inside.

Farther down the sidewalk, she saw a group of young women walking. They cast sad glances at the apartment building.

"Hey, Officer Brown," Brynn said.

"Detective Sullivan." The cop nodded at her.

"Is Detective Morgan inside?"

The young man nodded. "He said for you to go straight up." The officer glanced at the idling SUV. "Hell of a guard dog you've got there, Detective."

She raised a brow. "Be careful, he bites."

Suddenly, a shot rang out.

Officer Brown jerked, blood spraying.

Shit. She grabbed him and yanked him down.

More bullets hit the building above their heads.

Shit. Shit. Shit.

Brynn slapped a hand on the officer's wound and pulled him toward the front door alcove.

"Oh, my God. Oh, my God." Brown's breathing was fast and panicked.

"Hey, stay calm." She checked his arm. "It doesn't look too bad."

His chest was heaving, but he managed a nod.

"Get inside," she said.

Another hail of gunfire hit. She scanned around the street. Multiple snipers, likely up on a roof somewhere.

She saw the door of the X6 open.

Bullets peppered the SUV. She gasped, her heart leaping into her throat. *God*. Vander.

She pulled her SIG. She had no target, but she fired in the direction of the rooftop across the street.

More bullets pinged into the X6.

Her gut tied itself into a knot. She knew the X6 had some armor, but it couldn't handle sustained gun fire.

It wouldn't protect Vander forever.

There. Movement on the building rooftop across the street. She fired again.

There was another barrage of gunfire aimed in her direction. She slid back into the alcove just as bits of brick flew everywhere.

Then she heard screams.

Dammit, the young women on the sidewalk.

No.

During a pause in the gunfire, Brynn peeked around the corner of her hiding place.

She saw the three women crouched on the ground, huddled together, with their hands clamped on their ears.

Someone was still firing on Vander, keeping him pinned.

Brynn took a deep breath, then she burst out of the doorway and ran toward the women.

"Up! Get off the street!" she yelled.

The women rose, blinking, their faces pale.

Brynn grabbed the arm of one. "Run into the nearest building."

All of a sudden, the throaty roars of engines echoed down the street. Brynn stiffened.

A pack of motorcycles roared into view, zipping and weaving.

Shit. "Go. Run!"

The women stumbled into a run, racing down the sidewalk. Brynn sprinted after them.

She glanced back and saw more bullets hit the X6. The windshield was a spider web of cracks.

Her chest tightened until it was painful. *Please be okay, Vander.*

Bullets hit the sidewalk ahead of them, and the women screamed and stopped.

Brynn aimed up at the rooftop. *Where the hell are you, asshole?*

She saw a flash of movement and fired.

A man slumped over the edge of the roof and she smiled grimly.

Someone heaved him back.

"Move!" she shouted again. "Get inside."

Two of the women sprinted toward the closest building.

Suddenly, a Harley roared onto the sidewalk. The third woman screamed, frozen to the spot.

More bikes pulled in closer. All the bikers wore bandanas over their faces.

A biker grabbed the third woman. She screamed.

"Let her go!" Brynn fired, just above the biker's head.

He released the woman, and Brynn yanked her away.

There were more gunshots, Harleys circling them. It was pure chaos.

Shit. She looked around.

"Across the street." Brynn pulled the woman's hand and yanked her into the street.

But the bikers were waiting.

As the bikes roared toward them, circling them like sharks, their engines roaring, Brynn's mouth went dry. She realized the bikers and the gunmen had been herding her right where they wanted her.

Brynn fired and one biker toppled off his bike. Another tried to grab the woman again, but Brynn pulled her away and fired again.

There. A break.

She shoved the woman. "Run. Get inside. As fast as you can!"

The woman took off running, her steps jerky. She almost tripped on the curb, but caught her balance, then sprinted into the closest building.

Brynn turned back and saw cops—led by Hunt—spilling out of the apartment building on the other side of the street.

Thank God.

Vander's X6 was still being peppered with bullets.

Suddenly, there was a deafening roar of a motorcycle. Brynn was already turning as she was yanked off her feet.

She struggled, and found herself thrown across a biker's lap. Her gun flew out of her hand.

The bike wheeled around, tires screeching, then sped down the street.

She fought, but he landed a hard punch to the back of her head and she saw stars.

"Hold still, or I'll enjoy hurting you."

Her insides froze. The wind rushed at her and she glanced up.

She recognized the voice and the glittering eyes over the red fabric of his bandana.

Nomad.

FUCK.

Vander gritted his teeth as more bullets hit the windshield and metalwork of the SUV.

A shattered web of cracks filled the windshield. He couldn't see Brynn anymore. The last he'd seen of her she was trying to save a terrified woman.

Fuck. He rammed a hand onto the steering wheel. He was pinned down. Nomad had planned this well. Keep Vander out of the picture, and lure Brynn out, because of course she'd run to save others.

He heard more gunfire and peered through his side window. He saw Hunt and several cops spill out onto the street.

Fuck this. Vander shoved open his door again.

And saw a biker yank Brynn onto his bike.

No. Vander's jaw locked.

He slammed the door shut and gunned the SUV's engine. He prayed the light armor built into the body was enough to keep the engine running.

He roared down the street. Bikers scattered, but one was too slow. Vander clipped him and the biker flew into the air, his Harley skidding away.

Vander didn't stop to watch. He kept his gaze through the cracked windshield, locked on the bike and Brynn.

Damn, he could barely see. As they turned a corner, traffic thickened. As they careened around another corner, he gritted his teeth.

He touched the dash. "Ace!"

"I'm here."

"Pull up Brynn's tracker. A biker has her and I'm in pursuit."

Vander grabbed his Glock, then slammed the butt against the windshield. Then again.

The shattered glass fell out. Air rushed at him, but at least he could see.

There they were.

He spotted the Harley zipping through the cars ahead. He saw the bike take a turn.

Vander jerked the wheel and followed. His heart was pounding, but he tried to stay focused. He had to get Brynn back. That was all he cared about.

Nomad was not fucking getting his hands on her.

Vander saw the bike mount the sidewalk, then turn another corner.

A car blocked Vander's way and he hit the brakes.

"Come on!" He leaned on the horn.

The car jerked forward, then slowly moved out of his way. He gunned the engine. He raced past, metal screeching as the X6 scraped the side of the other vehicle.

He turned onto the street. There were several cars and a delivery truck, but no bike.

"Ace! I don't have a visual."

"The tracker shows her five hundred feet ahead of you. They're still moving."

Vander accelerated and scanned. He overtook another car.

"I don't see a bike."

"They should be right there," Ace said.

Dammit. "I don't see her." *No. Fucking, no.*

He kept driving, following the flow of traffic.

"They've turned! They're moving away from you. Southeast toward 101."

Cursing, Vander yanked the wheel. He sped on, looking for any sign of the Harley.

Nothing.

Trucks, cars, cabs, but no bike.

No Brynn.

"Fuck, Vander," Ace said. "They're on the highway. They're heading south and picking up speed."

Vander slammed his palm on the wheel. He wouldn't catch them now.

"Come back to Norcross," Ace said. "We'll see where they take her, and plan a rescue op."

Vander ground his teeth together. Every second that Nomad had her, was a second the asshole could hurt her.

A flashback reared in his head. Two of his team taken hostage by the Taliban.

Neither had made it.

Vander had rescued them, but he'd been too late. All that had been left were lumps of meat.

He kept a tenuous grip on his control as he drove back to the office. Several of his tires were flat, and the engine was whining as it died. He drove into the parking level.

Saxon and Hunt were waiting. They took one look at his face and flinched.

"We're going to get her back," Hunt growled.

Vander gave the man a curt nod. "Did you arrest any bikers at the scene?"

"Yes, but no one's talking."

"The women on the street?"

"Safe. Shaken, but not hurt. And our officer is fine too."

They strode upstairs and straight into Ace's office. Rhys was there, leaning against the wall. He nodded, a promise in his eyes. Vander was unsurprised to see Easton there as well, in an expensive, tailored suit, his face serious. He nodded as well.

His brothers, his men, they would never let him down.

Vander blew out a breath.

"I found out how Nomad evaded us," Ace said.

On-screen was some CCTV of the streets near where Brynn was snatched. Vander saw cars driving past, then a blue delivery truck came into view. As Vander watched, the back of the truck opened downward, forming a ramp. Then a Harley—ridden by a biker and a struggling woman—rode right up inside the truck. The ramp closed and the truck picked up speed.

A moment later, Vander's battered X6 sped past.

His blood boiled. He'd driven straight past the truck. Driven straight past Brynn and he hadn't even known. *Fuck.*

Saxon gripped his shoulder. "Lock it down. She needs your head in the game."

Rhys nodded. "You're the best fucking commander Ghost Ops ever had. You can plan a rescue op better than any man I know."

Vander dragged in air, and looked at Ace. "They stopped moving yet?"

"Not yet. But it looks like they're heading to the port. They're pulling in at Pier 94. That's the bulk terminal, where sands and aggregates are unloaded."

On another screen, Vander saw the delivery truck driving into the port facility. There were several large cranes in the distance, and long piles of gray sand.

Vander frowned. Why the hell was Nomad taking Brynn there? He guessed it was a deserted, out-of-the-way place for torture and murder.

"Maybe Nomad has a warehouse there," Hunt suggested.

"We need to start planning the rescue," Saxon said.

As his friends talked, their words turned to a drone. Vander stared at the screen. Was she scared? Was she hurt?

He blew out a breath. *No.* She'd be fighting. She'd be holding on for him to get there.

Vander prayed he wasn't too late.

"They've stopped," Ace barked.

Vander looked at the glowing dot on the screen.

"Wait." Ace tapped. "What the hell?"

Vander watched the dot move...into the water of the Bay.

"They're on a boat?" Hunt asked.

"To where?" Rhys asked.

"Pull up the satellite image," Vander ordered.

A satellite image filled the screen, showing the water of the Bay, and several bulk carrier ships docked there.

"They're heading for a ship," Hunt breathed.

"I suspect that's how Nomad's been getting Stardust into the city," Vander said.

"There." Ace pointed to a ship. "They've stopped there." He tapped the keyboard. "A ship called the *Reliance Express.* Last port of call—" he looked up "—Port of Lázaro Cárdenas, Mexico."

Vander stared at the dot. *Hold on, Brynn. I'm coming.* "All right. We know where she is." He marched out of the room.

"Where are you going?" Hunt asked.

"To get my gear together so I can get my woman back."

CHAPTER NINETEEN

B rynn climbed the ladder up the side of the ship. The biker behind her gave her a vicious shove.

She looked down and glared at him.

"Move it," Nomad barked from above.

She pulled herself onto the deck of the cargo ship, and saw Nomad talking with some of the ship's crew. They all had blank-faced looks that said they had no interest in getting involved in anyone else's business.

She'd get no help there.

Brynn kept her face blank. She wouldn't give Nomad the satisfaction of seeing her fear. They had no idea that she was wearing a tracker.

Vander would come.

She just had to hold out until then.

She scanned the flat deck of the ship. It was a bulk carrier, so she saw the huge covers over each of the holds. She swallowed. Nomad had no doubt been using shipping connections to bring his drugs in.

She got shoved again and they walked inside the

raised tower at the back of the ship. She knew the bridge would be at the top, various accommodation levels in the center, and the engine rooms beneath. They moved into a tight corridor.

Nomad led them down some stairs, down another narrow corridor, and into a room.

It was some sort of cabin with no windows and tight quarters. She was shoved into a chair and her hands roughly tied behind her back.

"So." Nomad paced in front of her. "I finally have you where I want you...Detective Sullivan."

She raised a brow. "It took you long enough to work out who I was, Tony."

He scowled, then quick as a snake, backhanded her on her already bruised face.

Ow. She bit her lip and tasted blood. Her eyes watered. "I've been doing some digging on you, Tony. I heard that your last motorcycle club wasn't happy with you. You kept wanting more, overstepping."

His mouth flattened. "I'm smart and take initiative. My boss appreciates that. He sent me here to expand the business."

Brynn made a scoffing sound. "He sent you here to get you out of his hair."

His jaw worked. He leaned over, grabbed the front of her shirt and twisted. "I will succeed here. I'm setting up the Stardust supply in San Francisco, and for icing on the cake, I'll hand my boss the head of Vander Norcross. I'll be a *legend*."

Brynn laughed. She leaned forward, laughing so hard that tears leaked out of her eyes.

Nomad stepped back, glaring at her.

"You... Think..." She kept laughing. "You think you can take Vander?" She snorted. "He's going to destroy you, piece by piece."

"No, he won't. Not when I have you. His weakness. What I'll do to you will break him."

She felt a skitter of raw fear but met his gaze head on. "You'll die today, Tony, regardless of what you do to me."

The biker just smiled. "I have a huge shipment of drugs on this ship. It's busy being packaged for distribution. I'm going to make you hurt, and then I'll watch Norcross lose his shit, get sloppy, and die from my bullet in his brain. Then I'll make lots of money." Nomad straightened. "Now, I need to go and check on my product."

He gripped her chin and she tried to yank free.

"I'm gonna let you sit here and wait until I'm ready to play with you, Detective Brynn Sullivan." He released her and strode to the door. "Watch her."

The two burly bikers near the door crossed their arms over their chests.

Brynn's stomach rolled. *Hurry, Vander.*

NIGHT HAD FALLEN.

This area of the port was quiet and shrouded in shadows.

Saxon, Rhys, Easton, and Hunt stood nearby. Ace had his computer set up near one of the X6s, tapping quickly.

Vander stared across the water. The lights of several ships glinted in the dark, but he focused on the *Reliance Express*.

He wore a black wetsuit. How many similar missions had he stood like this, readying to go into battle? Usually he'd be calm, using his nerves to fuel him.

But the stakes on this mission were high.

Brynn.

She was his. His confident, smart ass, courageous detective.

He sucked in a breath and stared at the ship again. It was a mile and a half offshore.

The others were dressed like him, talking out the plan.

Vander turned. "I'm going alone."

"What?" Hunt barked.

Saxon frowned. "Vander—"

"Hunt, you aren't trained for a water assault. Saxon, you're well aware that the more of us who go in, the more likely they'll spot us. That increases the chance that Nomad will kill her."

The men all scowled. Rhys put his hands on his hips. "You can't go alone. What if you need backup?"

"I'll have it." He glanced across the water. "Brynn."

"Vander, it's almost two miles to swim in the dark," Hunt said.

Rhys coughed. "That's a walk in the park for Vander. He can do that in his sleep."

"I've hacked the ship's systems," Ace said. "They have a couple of CCTV cameras. No sign of Brynn. I can see lots of movement and lighting on. Best I can guess, she's likely one deck down, starboard side. Just above the engine room."

Vander nodded. "If you see anything else let me know."

Ace nodded. "Sure thing."

"Jesus." Hunt swept a hand through his hair. "Our family is in chaos. They're all worried."

And Hunt was worried. There were deep grooves on either side of his mouth.

"I'm bringing her home." Vander's voice vibrated with dark promise. He'd get her off that ship, even if he didn't make it back.

Hunt stared at him for a long beat, then nodded. "Bring her home."

Vander shouldered a small, waterproof backpack with his Glock inside and a few other goodies.

He had a knife strapped to his thigh and a few other things hidden.

He nodded at his friends.

Then he dove into the water cleanly. The cool water seeped around him, but his suit offered him good protection. He kept Norcross Security well-stocked with top-of-the-line gear.

He rose and looked at his friends.

"Good hunting," Rhys said.

Saxon and Easton nodded.

Hunt met his gaze. "Bring our girl home."

"I'm going to tell her that you called her a girl," Vander said.

Hunt's lips quirked, but he still looked grim. Vander

knew that Hunt would welcome a punch or sharp barb from Brynn right now.

Vander stuck his expensive, experimental rebreather in his mouth, then sank into the water.

Cold silent darkness closed around him. He kicked powerfully, heading toward the *Reliance Express*.

He focused on stealth, careful not to leave any ripples or splashes.

I'm coming, Brynn.

HER ARMS WERE GOING NUMB.

Brynn subtly kept working to loosen the ropes on her wrists.

The two bikers weren't paying her much attention, talking trash to each other, and occasionally sending scowls or leers her way.

Nomad hadn't returned.

She felt a slight bit of give in the rope and kept working.

"The man's got plans for you, Princess," the biker with a large gut and long hair said.

Princess? *Ugh*

"Oh, yeah. He's gonna mess you up." The other biker was younger, and high on something. He was filled with nervous energy and couldn't stand still, occasionally tugging on his shaggy, dirty-blond hair.

"He'll let us help mess you up," the older biker guffawed.

"Charming. You good guys will have such a great time when I lock you in a cell."

They both laughed.

"You're tied to a chair, Princess. When we're done with you, that man of yours won't even touch you."

Her stomach rolled, but she kept her gaze bored.

"Yeah, Nomad likes to brand people," the younger one said, ugly excitement in his voice. "He's got a way with a hot rod."

The other man laughed. "And he doesn't just stick to the outside."

Brynn hid her grimace. Just when she thought these assholes couldn't get any worse.

She redoubled her effort to loosen the rope and get free. She couldn't just wait for Vander.

She needed to get off this ship.

The rope released.

Yes.

She freed one wrist, then the other. She was careful not to alert her captors. She rotated her shoulders gently, getting some feeling back into her tingling arms.

Right. Now she needed to deal with Tweedledee and Tweedledum.

"She's a hot piece." The younger biker moved closer.

Yes, come a little closer.

As the biker sauntered toward her, she gripped the length of rope in her hands.

She tried to look nervous, and swallowed a few times.

That just made him smile. He twitched again, then touched her leg, sliding it up her thigh.

"I'm a leg man. You have nice ones."

"Sorry, I like my men a little taller, stronger, and smarter."

His brow creased. The older biker chuckled.

Fury filled the younger guy's face. His body twitched again. "You'll like me just fine, baby, when I shove my cock in you." He leaned in. "I might start with my tongue down your throat, for a little taste."

"Blue, don't get too close to her," the older biker warned. "She's Nomad's."

"I'm not gonna make her bleed. Yet."

His hot, unpleasant breath washed over her face.

Brynn exhaled slowly, then she whipped her hands up and snapped the rope around his neck.

Blue's eyes went comically wide.

"Sorry, you're just not my type," she said.

She surged up out of her chair, and yanked the rope on both ends. It went taut and he choked. He clawed at his neck.

She rammed into him and he stumbled back. She kept the rope tight, and kicked him. He slammed into the wall.

She pulled harder, and his face started to turn purple. Then she heard a roar behind her.

Brynn dodged to the side, and the older biker slammed into his friend with a grunt. Blue slid down the wall.

Brynn grabbed the chair she'd been tied to, and swung it.

It slammed into the older biker's face with a crunch. Wood splintered.

He bellowed and rushed her. A giant fist swung at her.

She ducked, then snatched up a broken arm of the chair and spun.

The biker, face twisted with anger, came at her again.

She ducked. Then she landed a solid front kick to his heavy gut. The air rushed out of him. She rammed the chair arm into his shoulder.

"Argh!"

As he staggered, she leaped up and executed a perfect roundhouse kick.

Her boot connected with his head.

He flew to the side and collapsed on top of his moaning friend. Quickly, Brynn used the rope to tie the men's hands together.

"Well, it's been a pleasure, boys. Sit tight. I'll have that cell ready for you in no time."

She swiveled. *Time to get out of here.*

She patted down the bikers and found a knife. Not much, but she could work with it.

Slowly, she opened the door and peered out. The corridor was empty.

She slipped out of the room.

Silently, she padded down the hall. She came to a junction. She wasn't exactly sure of the quickest way out.

Suddenly, she heard echoing voices getting closer.

Crap.

She turned and opened the closest door. It was a small cabin, thankfully empty, with a narrow bunk, and built-in desk and cupboard. She slipped inside.

Leaning against the wall, she waited, the door ajar

the tiniest fraction. A moment later, two men—sailors by the looks of them—walked past her.

She released a breath, then slipped back out.

Get to the top deck, get off the ship, then swim to shore. *Nothing to it.*

Then she heard something and paused.

What was that?

Her gut churned. It had been the smallest scrape of sound, but now she heard nothing. Her mouth went dry. She didn't hear anything, but she just knew someone was close. She was also well aware that at any moment, Nomad could be back and find her missing.

She needed to be off the ship before that happened.

She heard a faint noise again. Was it a footstep?

It didn't matter. She needed to go.

She lifted the pocketknife and hurried down the corridor. Now, she just needed—

A body in black came around the corner and she collided with the man. Hard arms closed around her.

Brynn whipped the knife up, and it took her half a second to register that she knew that wet body pressed against her. She knew it intimately.

"Vander!"

He cupped her cheeks, then kissed her.

God. The fear leaked out of her. He'd come. Just as she'd known he would.

He broke the kiss. "Are you okay?"

She nodded, and took in his damp wetsuit. "You swum out here?"

He nodded.

God, her man. He was totally in love with her.

244

"Let's go," she said. "I left two groaning bikers back there, and Nomad will find them soon."

Something moved through his eyes. "I come to rescue you, but of course, you've rescued yourself." He stroked her cheekbone.

"What did you expect me to do?"

He gave a slight shake of his head. "Come on."

His strong hand grabbed hers, squeezed, then released her. She knew he needed his hands free.

All of a sudden, shouts echoed through the ship.

Uh-oh. She was pretty sure someone had discovered Blue and his friend.

"Move," Vander said urgently.

She followed him, moving fast. He paused, and held up a fist. Voices were coming down the corridor to their left.

Shit.

He swiveled and they backtracked. They raced down another passageway, and passed another junction.

"Wait," she whispered. "There are stairs down that way."

He turned back and peered down the cross passage. But a second later, several bikers spilled into the corridor.

"Vander!" she yelled.

He was already moving. His brutal punches and kicks were a blur.

Soon, the bikers were all writhing on the ground, groaning.

She grinned. So badass.

Then she felt a gun barrel at the back of her neck and froze.

"Drop your weapons, Norcross," Nomad said from behind her. "She won't be so attractive with a bullet hole in her head."

Vander rose in that sleek wetsuit that emphasized his muscular frame.

"Drop your weapons," Nomad said again.

Vander pulled out his Glock and the knife off his thigh.

"Vander, no," she said.

The gun barrel jammed harder into her flesh and she winced.

Vander dropped his weapons on the floor.

CHAPTER TWENTY

Vander gritted his teeth as his bound arms were hauled above his head.

"You're going to regret this, Nomad," Brynn spat. She twisted, but the big biker who was her captor held her still.

Beside her, Nomad watched with a smile on his face.

They were in the engine room, deep in the bowels of the ship. Three men were holding Vander, throwing the rope binding him over some overhead pipework. They hauled him up until he felt the strain in his shoulders and his toes barely touched the floor.

"I'll be quite the legend in San Francisco. Taking down the infamous Vander Norcross." Nomad stepped forward. "You aren't so tough. I think you've greatly exaggerated your skills."

Vander just lifted his head and stared at the man. "I don't need to exaggerate anything. And I don't go around talking about my greatness like some people."

The man's face twisted. He punched Vander in the gut.

Air whooshed out of Vander and he jerked against the ropes.

"Oh, you're so tough, Tony," Brynn said. "You'll only fight him when he's tied up."

Damn, she was magnificent. Her hair with all its strands of colors framed her face. He could see that she was hiding her fear, not giving up.

The door to the room opened and a biker strode in, carrying a bag. He set it down on the table and Nomad strode over, an eager look on his face.

He opened the bag, and pulled out a long metal bar and a blowtorch. He turned the torch on, and stuck the end of the metal rod in the flame.

Vander saw Brynn stiffen.

"Detective Sullivan," the man said. "Please remove the top of your man's wetsuit."

She lifted her chin. "No."

The biker behind her shoved her hard, then followed through with a slap to her face.

Vander jerked against his bindings.

Nomad nodded at his bag. Another biker reached in and pulled out a large pair of scissors. He shoved them into Brynn's hand.

"You try to use those as a weapon—" Nomad lifted the blowtorch higher "—and I'll use this on you first, starting with that face of yours."

One hand cupping her cheek and the other clenching the scissors, she straightened and walked toward Vander.

Now he saw the fear in her eyes. Her freckles were stark against her skin.

"Vander..." she whispered.

There was that blend he loved so much—strength and softness. He saw her fear, but under it was the steel that would hold her together.

She reached up for the fastening of his wetsuit, then slowly opened the zipper.

"It'll be okay," he murmured.

She bit her lip, then lifted the scissors. Her jaw was clenched tight as she cut through the neoprene. With his arms bound, she couldn't slide the sleeves off, so she cut through the fabric.

Finally, she pushed the top half of his suit off, baring his chest.

She touched his skin, tracing the inked words on his pec.

"Freedom is never free," she whispered.

"Trust me," he said.

"I do, but..."

Yeah, the situation looked bad. "I vow to get you out of here safely. I won't let anyone touch you, hurt you—" his tone lowered, and he let what he felt show through "—or take you from me."

She swallowed.

"I came alone because I told my guys that I had all the backup I needed, right here."

Her pretty pale-blue eyes flared. She nodded.

"Get back." A biker grabbed the back of her shirt and yanked her backward. Vander saw her hands clench—

one on the scissors and one into a fist—and he knew that she wanted to strike.

But his detective was smart.

She slid the scissors down by her side and out of view.

Nomad turned. The rod in his hand was glowing red at one end.

"Let us go and I won't kill you all," Vander said.

The bikers all laughed.

Nomad smiled. He moved the burning hot brand around. "You'll be screaming shortly. I love seeing marks branded deep into skin. It's an art. And the scent of burning flesh is so primal."

"You're a pig," Brynn snapped.

Nomad glanced her way. "Your lovely skin will look beautiful covered in my marks, Detective."

Vander's muscles strained. He fought not to react, grinding his teeth together. "Last warning, Nomad."

The biker shook his head. "Stubborn. You just can't see the writing on the wall." He strode closer.

Vander sucked in a breath, then released it slowly.

Nomad stepped in front of him.

Vander flexed his abs, and lifted his feet. He kicked the branding rod out of the man's hands, and it flew away, clattering to the floor.

Nomad shouted and Vander landed a savage kick to the man's head. He flew back and crashed to the floor.

Two bikers rushed at Vander. He kicked one, who staggered into the other. His next kick was direct to the man's nose and blood sprayed.

The slimmer of the two charged, and Vander got his

legs around the guy's neck. Before the man could do anything, Vander tightened his grip and squeezed his legs, trapping the man in a chokehold.

The guy struggled, but Vander tightened his grip and held on. A moment later, the biker sagged, and Vander dropped him.

Vander lifted his legs all the way up. He saw Brynn fighting with the big biker. She got in a good front kick and a punch.

Vander managed to pull his hidden knife from his boot with his bound hands. It was awkward, but in Ghost Ops, they'd practiced loads of situations like this. They were always tying each other up and trying to get free.

Carefully, so he didn't drop the knife or cut himself, he started sawing on the rope.

The knife was very sharp.

A second later, the ropes fell and Vander dropped to the floor in a crouch.

He yanked the remaining ropes off, just as Brynn slammed the biker into the wall and rammed her elbow into his neck.

Gagging, he slid down the wall.

She spun, saw Vander free, and blinked.

Then she smiled. "You are so badass."

They both moved, and collided together. Their kiss was hot and hungry.

"I know it's so wrong, but I'm so turned on right now," she said.

Vander hugged her tighter. "You are something else, Detective."

"You too, Norcross." She looked past him, her eyes widening. He spun.

It was no new bad guy.

But there was a fire.

Flames were dancing up the wall.

"Fuck." The brand must've ignited something. "Come on."

He took her hand and they ran. They exited the room and sprinted down the corridor.

They passed a group of bewildered sailors.

"Fire!" Brynn yelled. "Evacuate."

They were almost to the top deck when an alarm started blaring. She saw sailors running all over the place.

The night air hit them.

Boom.

The ship rocked beneath their feet.

Vander pulled her to the railing and looked at her. "Trust me?"

"Always."

There was another boom and some of the hatch covers blew upward, flames shooting into the night sky.

Vander tightened his hold on Brynn's fingers, then they leaped off the side of the ship and into the water.

BRYNN KICKED TO THE SURFACE, spitting out water. She circled her legs, watching as Vander came up right beside her.

They both looked back at the burning ship, watching sailors jump into the water.

"Nice rescue," she said.

"The exploding ship part was an added bonus." He circled an arm around her and kissed her.

She wasn't sure how long they stayed there, holding each other and kissing in the water. It was the roar of a boat engine that made them separate.

She looked up, just as a bright beam of light hit them. A sleek speedboat raced closer.

It slowed and circled around them.

"Here we are," Saxon drawled from the bow of the boat. "Worried you both just exploded, and you're making out."

"Screw you, Buchanan," Vander said, no heat in his tone.

Hunt was at the speedboat's controls.

Saxon pulled them aboard. Brynn was sopping wet, and when the cool breeze hit her, she shivered.

Then her cousin wrapped his arms around her and hugged her.

"I'm all right," she said.

Hunt looked at Vander. "Thank you."

Vander shrugged a shoulder. "She was already partway through rescuing herself."

She grinned.

Her cousin shook his head.

Vander pulled her close. Saxon found a blanket and Vander draped it around them. He sat down, pulling her onto his lap, and wrapping his arms tightly around her. Like he never wanted to let go.

Brynn was fine with that.

She pressed a hand to his damp, bare chest, her palm

against his beating heart. As they headed back toward the shore, they passed several police boats speeding toward the burning ship.

As they neared the port, she saw lights, cars, and a crowd.

"Brace yourselves," Saxon warned. "The gang and the families have all descended."

Among the crowd, Brynn saw her mom, her sisters, and her brother. She groaned.

Vander just held her tighter. Hunt slowed the speed-boat and they came to a stop alongside the pier. Saxon tied it off and Vander helped her off the boat.

"Brynn!" She was engulfed by her mom. Then her sisters were there, babbling and hugging her.

Bard looked freaked. He glanced at the burning ship in the Bay, then back at her. "Jesus, Brynn."

"I'm okay."

He nudged their younger sister aside and hugged her.

Then she was tugged away. Vander pulled her tight to his side, his face warning her not to argue.

Her sisters stared at him.

"Wow." Carrin's eyes went wide.

Naomi's lips formed an O.

Gia, Easton, and the rest of the Norcross gang were behind him. They didn't look upset at all. They must be used to this kind of action-fueled drama.

"Brynn!" Mrs. Norcross moved forward and hugged her.

Mr. Norcross appeared and patted her shoulder. He winked. "Thanks for looking out for my son."

"We looked after each other," Brynn said.

Vander slid an arm around her shoulders. "Can I have my woman back now?"

"Wait." Bard looked shocked, and a little green. "You're Vander Norcross." He turned to Brynn. "You're sleeping with Vander Norcross? Are you insane?"

She bristled. "No, Bard, I'm in love with Vander Norcross."

The crowd went quiet, and Vander's grip tightened on her. She turned her head to look up at him.

"And he's in love with me." She didn't look away from his dark gaze. "You're in love with me."

He just stared, but she saw his bare, muscled chest rising and falling.

Her heart clutched. *Come on, Vander.* "Do you have the guts to tell me how you feel?"

She was excruciatingly conscious of their audience glancing between them.

"I warned you that relationships aren't for a man like me," he said.

Someone let out an angry hiss. Brynn thought it was Gia.

Brynn made a scoffing sound. "Come on, Vander. Everything you do is for your family, your friends, your employees. Those are all relationships. You're big, badass, and tough on the outside, the ultimate protector. But underneath, you're all soft and gooey."

There were several gasps from the audience.

A muscle flexed in his jaw "Brynn—"

"You take care of everyone. You've helped them get their businesses started. You go all out to help the women they fall in love with. And I know that you help returning vets integrate into civilian life. I investigated you too. I know just how much money and time you funnel into the Returning Warriors charity. I know that you started it, all quiet and anonymous."

His mouth firmed. "None of that matters—"

"Oh, yes it does. You're so in love with me you can't think straight."

He stared at her and didn't say anything.

The silence stretched on.

Her heart caved in, and suddenly the adrenaline of the night crashed in on her. God, what if he could never deal with his feelings? She was standing here, baring her heart to him, and he was still protecting himself.

She scraped a hand through her wet hair. "I guess there is something that Vander Norcross is afraid of." She turned away. "I just want to go home."

Vander surged forward and grabbed her with a growl. "Will you let me talk?"

"I don't—"

He kissed her. It was hard, intense, and filled with feeling. He slid his hand into her wet hair. Of course, even though she was tired and angry, it was Vander, so she kissed him back.

When he lifted his mouth, she was surprised her eyes didn't roll back and her legs collapse.

"I've never loved a woman before. Never wanted to, never came anywhere close to love. So, a little patience, please."

Her heart took off like a race horse. "Oh."

"I told you that I'd never let you go. You're mine. I'm yours. Your home is with *me*. Nobody's ever going to love you as much as I do. Nobody will feel what I feel for you."

She melted. She didn't feel cold anymore. "Oh, Vander."

It was so Vander and it was perfect.

His mouth took hers again.

There was clapping and cheering. Brynn heard Mrs. Norcross crying. When she lifted her head, she saw Vander's mom leaning against her husband. Brynn's mom and sisters were smiling. Bard's face was blank. Oh well, he'd adjust.

"Poor Jack never stood a chance," Naomi said.

Vander gripped Brynn's jaw and she looked back at him.

"I want marriage and babies," he said.

She jerked. "Right now?"

That got her one of those gorgeous smiles. "No, but soon you'll wear my ring, and one day, you'll have my babies."

"You're supposed to ask, Vander."

"I will. Eventually. When the time's right." He pressed a quick kiss to her lips and then ran his thumb along her cheekbone. "For now, you're moving in with me."

Another order. She rolled her eyes. "Ask me."

"Brynn, will you make a home with me?"

"*Yes.*"

They kissed again and she didn't care that they were surrounded by people and smelled like dirty water. She was right where she wanted to be.

CHAPTER TWENTY-ONE

Two months later

Vander strode into the alley. Suddenly, a teenage boy came barreling down from the other direction, looking back behind him.

Vander stuck his foot out and the boy tripped, face planting into the dirty concrete. The handbag he was clutching flew out of his hand.

"What the fuck?" The boy looked up, saw Vander, and froze. The color leached out of his face. "Ah...Norcross."

"You thought I wouldn't catch you?" Vander crouched and grabbed the handbag. "Get up. You're going to return this to the old lady you just mugged right in front of me. And apologize."

The gangbanger-in-training rose, swallowing.

Footsteps.

Vander turned and saw two big silhouettes.

"That boy's one of ours." One man stepped forward. He was covered in tattoos with a shaved head.

"Yeah, we're gonna make you pay, motherfucker," the other gang member said. He was shorter, muscular, missing a front tooth, and had a hard look to his face. "You attack one Blade, you deal with all of us."

"These guys with you?" Vander asked the kid.

The boy nodded. "Just came up from LA."

"You don't answer to him," one of the men barked. "You want to be a Blade, you man up. *No one* orders us around."

"I suggest not being a Blade," Vander said to the boy.

"That's it, asshole." The man with the tattoos advanced.

"Tank, you shouldn't—" the kid started.

Vander attacked.

He landed a kick, ducked, then slammed a punch into the gangbanger's gut. The air rushed out of him. Vander grabbed the guy's shirt, then slammed him against the brick wall.

He turned to face the second Blade. With a cry, the guy rushed him.

Vander sidestepped, and caught the man in a headlock. He hammered a punch into the guy's face. The man's body sagged and Vander tossed him on the ground beside the other groaning Blade member.

He turned to the teenager.

The boy was wiping his hands on his jeans, gaping at the two downed gang members.

He met Vander's gaze. "I want to be like you."

"Go to school, kid. Avoid the gangs. Join the military. Fight to protect people, not hurt them."

Unhurried, sure footsteps echoed down the alley.

Vander and the kid looked up.

Brynn stepped out of the shadows wearing what he thought of as her cop uniform—dark jeans, boots, a white shirt, and a fitted, navy-blue jacket. Her badge glinted where it was hooked onto her belt, and her hair was up in a ponytail. He knew she'd been in court today.

"Cop," the kid whispered. "Hot cop."

"Hello, Detective," Vander drawled.

It hit him in the chest every time he saw her—everything he felt for her. It never dimmed, only grew stronger.

"Norcross. Fighting in dark alleys with shady characters, I see."

He smiled and handed the handbag to the boy. "Return it. Apologize."

The teenager nodded rapidly, then took the bag. He skated around Brynn and jogged out of the alley.

She looked at the groaning men on the ground. "You have a present for me?"

"All yours." He stepped closer and ran a hand down the lapel of her jacket.

"You know it gets me hot and bothered when you're all badass," she said.

"I know." He lowered his head and kissed that mouth he loved.

He was so damn in love with her. She made every day a little brighter, a little easier.

And every night, he slept tangled up with her.

He would never give up the tangles for anything.

"What time will you be home?" she asked.

"I'll try not to be late, but I have a meeting with Trucker."

Trucker had pulled through, and Vander had convinced the man to retire. Some decent members of the Iron Wanderers had taken over, and were cleaning up the club.

"And one other thing I need to take care of," he added.

"Remember we have the cook out at your parents' place," Brynn said.

"I know. Ma's already told me that she's making lasagna, even though Dad's grilling."

Brynn moaned. "I love your mother's lasagna. I gain two pounds every time we eat there."

He slid a hand down to her ass. "No complaints here."

She nipped his jaw. "All right. If you're late, I'll meet you at your parents' place. Now, let me call for some uniforms to pick up your two friends here." She smiled. "Love you."

Vander slid his nose down hers. "I love you too, Detective."

———

BRYNN SIPPED her beer and smiled.

Cook outs at Mr. and Mrs. Norcross's were awesome. She'd been over here for dinner quite a few times.

Vander's father was manning the grill, and Rhys was helping him. Mrs. Norcross was bustling in and out of the cute Edwardian house in Noe Valley. It was where Vander and his siblings grew up. Nearby, Brynn's mom and sisters were sitting with Gia at a table, smiling and chatting.

God, Dad, I wish you were here. He'd love Vander, and his family.

Brynn absorbed the bittersweet grief. He knew. In her heart, she knew he was looking over them and that he was proud.

Lights were strung up, giving the small backyard a festive feel. She spotted Ace and Maggie, and smiled. The woman had a big baby bump now, and Ace was stroking it. The helicopter pilot was glowing.

Vander was due to arrive soon. His meeting with Trucker had run late. The biker had retired, and Grill had left town for parts unknown. There was a new president at the Iron Wanderers, and last she'd heard, he was making their fight nights safe and legal, and opening the bar to the public. They were also going to ramp up the custom garage work.

Nomad and his goons hadn't made it off the *Reliance Express*. They'd gone down in the Bay with the ship and their drugs. Brynn wasn't very sorry about it.

She'd stopped the flood of Stardust into San Francisco. Satisfaction filled her. Far fewer young people were going to die from needless overdoses.

Anyway, enough work for tonight. She glanced over and saw Ryder talking with Sofie. Her cousin and the princess got on well. Sofie's handsome man Rome was with them, nodding at whatever Ryder was saying.

Haven and Harlow were drinking cocktails at the

edge of the deck with Mike Jankowski of all people. The detective had healed up just fine, although he was still on light duties at work. Bard was talking Easton's ear off. No doubt getting investment tips. Her brother was slowly coming around to the idea that his sister was living with Vander Norcross.

For a man who loved solitude, Vander was awesome to live with. He brought her coffee in the mornings, called or messaged her a few times throughout the day, and did the lion's share of the cooking. They loved lying on the couch together watching a game—ice hockey, baseball, football, they liked them all. He loved when she got riled up, shouting at the refs. He usually pounced on her afterward.

Lazy Sunday breakfast on his killer roof terrace had become their thing. Vander had a secret waffle and maple syrup obsession.

She fell more in love with him every day.

And every day, he spoke a little bit more about Ghost Ops with her. Not the classified details, but about the men and women he'd served with.

He was hers. *Completely.*

She saw Hunt walk in, loosening his tie. He had a rather impressive scowl on his face.

She snagged a bottle out of the ice-filled bucket on the deck and strode over. "Hey, need a beer?"

"Yeah."

"You look tired."

Her cousin's scowl deepened. "Thanks to my new neighbor. They play their music too loud, at all hours of the day and night."

"Oh." Brynn smiled. "Surely a visit from the friendly neighborhood detective should sort that out."

"She's hard to pin down." He sipped his beer. "Every time I knock, she's not home or doesn't answer."

"She?" *Interesting.* Brynn narrowed her gaze on Hunt's face. He seemed way more bent out of shape about this than her normally solid, in-control cousin should be.

"There's something off about her. She sticks to herself. She's cautious. There's a story there, and I don't trust her."

"*Mmm.*" Brynn saw the interest in her cousin's eyes. This looked much deeper than just a curious cop who didn't like loud music. "What's she look like?"

"I don't know. Five foot five, slim build, blonde hair with a bit of a curl."

In other words, he knew in great detail. "Did you run her?"

"Of course, I did. Clean as a whistle. Too clean."

Brynn raised a brow. "You think her ID is fake?"

He took another sip of his beer. "If it is, it's good."

Hunt was on the trail now. Her cousin was stubborn, and he wouldn't give up until he had answers.

She hoped his new neighbor wasn't a serial killer in hiding.

Two men stepped out of the house onto the deck and warmth filled her.

As always, her man looked hot. Vander was wearing jeans, and a button-down shirt in deep green that she'd bought for him. He scanned the crowd, and his gaze locked on her. He smiled.

Everything inside her fluttered.

Yes. More in love with him every day.

She glanced at the man beside him, and it took a second to recognize the tough, muscled man with buzzed brown hair.

"Camden!" she cried.

"What?" Hunt spun, his face lighting up. "Cam."

Hunt hugged his brother and they slapped each other's backs. Ryder cruised in for a hug as well.

"I thought you weren't back until next week," Hunt said.

Camden shrugged one broad shoulder. "Decided to ditch the beach and come home."

Brynn stepped up to him. "Hey, there."

"Brynn." He gave her a faint smile and a quick hug.

His pale green eyes looked flat and he had a new scar that ran down his cheek. It was healing, but still looked a little raw. He had a hard, unforgiving edge to him that hadn't been there before.

Her heart tripped. *Oh, Cam, what did you survive?*

"Can I have my woman, please?"

Camden released her and looked at Vander. "I don't know. She smells real good." Cam met her gaze. "I can't believe you shacked up with Norcross." A faint smile tried to break through.

"Best thing I ever did," she said. "It took me a while to knock some sense into him so that he finally admitted that he was crazy about me."

Vander grabbed her, snaked an arm around her waist, then kissed her until she was breathless.

"Trouble," he said. "Knew it from the moment I first met you." But he was smiling. "The best kind."

"Let's get you a beer, Cam," Hunt said.

Brynn watched her cousins, worry worming through her. Cam seemed so...hard, grim.

Vander stroked a hand down her back. "We'll take care of him."

"I know."

"He starts work at Norcross Security next week."

She nodded. It would be the best place for him. Surrounded by people who'd done the same things he had and come home.

"Come with me." Vander threaded his fingers through hers and led her down onto the grass, under the lights. "We used to lie out here when we were kids. We'd make a wish on any star that was bright enough to see."

She smiled at the thought of Vander being that young and innocent.

"I never dreamed of a woman I'd love so much that sometimes I just watch her sleeping."

Her insides turned to goo. "Vander—"

"Who makes me feel so damn much every day, especially when life had left me numb." He cupped her cheek. "You woke me up, Brynn."

"I love you so much, Vander."

"I know. You show me every day." He pulled something out of his pocket, then flicked open the lid of the small box.

She gasped, couldn't breathe.

The ring was gorgeous. A large, sparkling diamond surrounded by a halo of smaller ones.

"You can't tell out here, but the center diamond is a very pale blue. Like your eyes."

A blue diamond. Rare, unique, and special. Her chest filled with warmth.

"I already warned you that I won't ever let you go," he continued. "So, what do you say about becoming Detective Brynn Norcross from now on?"

She looked away from the ring and locked her gaze on his. "I say yes."

He slid the ring onto her finger and she was surprised to see his hand shake a little. Another little tell that showed her just how he felt about her.

Then he swept her up against him, lifting her off her feet. He kissed her under the lights, and shouts and whistles broke out from the deck.

Breathless, they turned their heads to see all their family and friends were at the deck railing, watching them and cheering.

"The dream I never knew I wanted came true," he murmured.

"And we've got more dreams to make, Vander. And a lot more tangles and complications."

"Bring it on, Detective." Then he kissed her again under the lights and stars.

I hope you enjoyed Vander and Brynn's story! I absolutely loved watching Vander take the fall.

This isn't the end for the Norcross gang! Stay tuned for

more Norcross Security next year. Hunt's story, **The Detective**, is coming in early 2022.

For more action romance, and little more Vander, check out the first book in the **Billionaire Heists trilogy**, *Stealing from Mr. Rich* (Zane Roth's story). **Read on for a preview of the first chapter.**

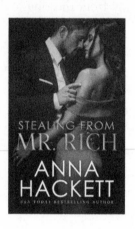

Don't miss out! For updates about new releases, free books, and other fun stuff, sign up for my VIP mailing list and get your *free box set* containing three action-packed romances.

Visit here to get started: www.annahackett.com

Would you like a FREE BOX SET of my books?

PREVIEW: STEALING FROM MR. RICH

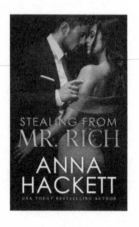

Monroe

The old-fashioned Rosengrens safe was a beauty.

I carefully turned the combination dial, then pressed closer to the safe. The metal was cool under my fingertips. The safe wasn't pretty, but stout and secure. There was something to be said for solid security.

Rosengrens had started making safes in Sweden over a hundred years ago. They were good at it. I listened to the pins, waiting for contact. Newer safes had internals made from lightweight materials to reduce sensory feedback, so I didn't get to use these skills very often.

Some people could play the piano, I could play a safe. The tiny vibration I was waiting for reached my fingertips, followed by the faintest click.

"I've gotcha, old girl." The Rosengrens had quite a few quirks, but my blood sang as I moved the dial again.

I heard a louder click and spun the handle.

The safe door swung open. Inside, I saw stacks of jewelry cases and wads of hundred-dollar bills. *Nice.*

Standing, I dusted my hands off on my jeans. "There you go, Mr. Goldstein."

"You are a doll, Monroe O'Connor. Thank you."

The older man, dressed neatly in pressed chinos and a blue shirt, grinned at me. He had coke-bottle glasses, wispy, white hair, and a wrinkled face.

I smiled at him. Mr. Goldstein was one of my favorite people. "I'll send you my bill."

His grin widened. "I don't know what I'd do without you."

I raised a brow. "You could stop forgetting your safe combination."

The wealthy old man called me every month or so to open his safe. Right now, we were standing in the home office of his expensive Park Avenue penthouse.

It was decorated in what I thought of as "rich, old man." There were heavy drapes, gold-framed artwork, lots of dark wood—including the built-in shelves around the safe—and a huge desk.

"Then I wouldn't get to see your pretty face," he said.

I smiled and patted his shoulder. "I'll see you next month, Mr. Goldstein." The poor man was lonely. His wife had died the year before, and his only son lived in Europe.

"Sure thing, Monroe. I'll have some of those donuts you like."

We headed for the front door and my chest tightened. I understood feeling lonely. "You could do with some new locks on your door. I mean, your building has top-notch security, but you can never be too careful. Pop by the shop if you want to talk locks."

He beamed at me and held the door open. "I might do that."

"Bye, Mr. Goldstein."

I headed down the plush hall to the elevator. Everything in the building screamed old money. I felt like an imposter just being in the building. Like I had "daughter of a criminal" stamped on my head.

Pulling out my cell phone, I pulled up my accounting app and entered Mr. Goldstein's callout. Next, I checked my messages.

Still nothing from Maguire.

Frowning, I bit my lip. That made it three days since I'd heard from my little brother. I shot him off a quick text.

"Text me back, Mag," I muttered.

The elevator opened and I stepped in, trying not to

worry about Maguire. He was an adult, but I'd practically raised him. Most days it felt like I had a twenty-four-year-old kid.

The elevator slowed and stopped at another floor. An older, well-dressed couple entered. They eyed me and my well-worn jeans like I'd crawled out from under a rock.

I smiled. "Good morning."

Yeah, yeah, I'm not wearing designer duds, and my bank account doesn't have a gazillion zeros. You're so much better than me.

Ignoring them, I scrolled through Instagram. When we finally reached the lobby, the couple shot me another dubious look before they left. I strode out across the marble-lined space and rolled my eyes.

During my teens, I'd cared about what people thought. Everyone had known that my father was Terry O'Connor—expert thief, safecracker, and con man. I'd felt every repulsed look and sly smirk at high school.

Then I'd grown up, cultivated some thicker skin, and learned not to care. *Fuck 'em.* People who looked down on others for things outside their control were assholes.

I wrinkled my nose. Okay, it was easier said than done.

When I walked outside, the street was busy. I smiled, breathing in the scent of New York—car exhaust, burnt meat, and rotting trash. Besides, most people cared more about themselves. They judged you, left you bleeding, then forgot you in the blink of an eye.

I unlocked my bicycle, and pulled on my helmet,

then set off down the street. I needed to get to the store. The ride wasn't long, but I spent every second worrying about Mag.

My brother had a knack for finding trouble. I sighed. After a childhood, where both our mothers had taken off, and Da was in and out of jail, Mag was entitled to being a bit messed up. The O'Connors were a long way from the Brady Bunch.

I pulled up in front of my shop in Hell's Kitchen and stopped for a second.

I grinned. *All mine.*

Okay, I didn't own the building, but I owned the store. The sign above the shop said *Lady Locksmith*. The logo was lipstick red—a woman's hand with gorgeous red nails, holding a set of keys.

After I locked up my bike, I strode inside. A chime sounded.

God, I loved the place. It was filled with glossy, warm-wood shelves lined with displays of state-of-the-art locks and safes. A key-cutting machine sat at the back.

A blonde head popped up from behind a long, shiny counter.

"You're back," Sabrina said.

My best friend looked like a doll—small, petite, with a head of golden curls.

We'd met doing our business degrees at college, and had become fast friends. Sabrina had always wanted to be tall and sexy, but had to settle for small and cute. She was my manager, and was getting married in a month.

"Yeah, Mr. Goldstein forgot his safe code again," I said.

Sabrina snorted. "That old coot doesn't forget, he just likes looking at your ass."

"He's harmless. He's nice, and lonely. How's the team doing?"

Sabrina leaned forward, pulling out her tablet. I often wondered if she slept with it. "Liz is out back unpacking stock." Sabrina's nose wrinkled. "McRoberts overcharged us on the Schlage locks again."

"That prick." He was always trying to screw me over. "I'll call him."

"Paola, Kat, and Isabella are all out on jobs."

Excellent. Business was doing well. Lady Locksmith specialized in providing female locksmiths to all the single ladies of New York. They also advised on how to keep them safe—securing locks, doors, and windows.

I had a dream of one day seeing multiple Lady Locksmiths around the city. Hell, around every city. A girl could dream. Growing up, once I understood the damage my father did to other people, all I'd wanted was to be respectable. To earn my own way and add to the world, not take from it.

"Did you get that new article I sent you to post on the blog?" I asked.

Sabrina nodded. "It'll go live shortly, and then I'll post on Insta, as well."

When I had the time, I wrote articles on how women —single *and* married—should secure their homes. My latest was aimed at domestic-violence survivors, and helping them feel safe. I donated my time to Nightingale House, a local shelter that helped women leaving DV situations, and I installed locks for them, free of charge.

"We should start a podcast," Sabrina said.

I wrinkled my nose. "I don't have time to sit around recording stuff." I did my fair share of callouts for jobs, plus at night I had to stay on top of the business-side of the store.

"Fine, fine." Sabrina leaned against the counter and eyed my jeans. "Damn, I hate you for being tall, long, and gorgeous. You're going to look *way* too beautiful as my maid of honor." She waved a hand between us. "You're all tall, sleek, and dark-haired, and I'm...the opposite."

I had some distant Black Irish ancestor to thank for my pale skin and ink-black hair. Growing up, I wanted to be short, blonde, and tanned. I snorted. "Beauty comes in all different forms, Sabrina." I gripped her shoulders. "You are so damn pretty, and your fiancé happens to think you are the most beautiful woman in the world. Andrew is gaga over you."

Sabrina sighed happily. "He does and he is." A pause. "So, do you have a date for my wedding yet?" My bestie's voice turned breezy and casual.

Uh-oh. I froze. All the wedding prep had sent my normally easygoing best friend a bit crazy. And I knew very well not to trust that tone.

I edged toward my office. "Not yet."

Sabrina's blue eyes sparked. "It's only *four* weeks away, Monroe. The maid of honor can't come alone."

"I'll be busy helping you out—"

"Find a date, Monroe."

"I don't want to just pick anyone for your wedding—"

Sabrina stomped her foot. "Find someone, or I'll find someone for you."

I held up my hands. "Okay, okay." I headed for my office. "I'll—" My cell phone rang. *Yes.* "I've got a call. Got to go." I dove through the office door.

"I won't forget," Sabrina yelled. "I'll revoke your best-friend status, if I have to."

I closed the door on my bridezilla bestie and looked at the phone.

Maguire. Finally.

I stabbed the call button. "Where have you been?"

"We have your brother," a robotic voice said.

My blood ran cold. My chest felt like it had filled with concrete.

"If you want to keep him alive, you'll do exactly as I say."

Zane

God, this party was boring.

Zane Roth sipped his wine and glanced around the ballroom at the Mandarin Oriental. The party held the Who's Who of New York society, all dressed up in their glittering best. The ceiling shimmered with a sea of crystal lights, tall flower arrangements dominated the tables, and the wall of windows had a great view of the Manhattan skyline.

Everything was picture perfect...and boring.

If it wasn't for the charity auction, he wouldn't be dressed in his tuxedo and dodging annoying people.

"I'm so sick of these parties," he muttered.

A snort came from beside him.

One of his best friends, Maverick Rivera, sipped his wine. "You were voted New York's sexiest billionaire bachelor. You should be loving this shindig."

Mav had been one of his best friends since college. Like Zane, Maverick hadn't come from wealth. They'd both earned it the old-fashioned way. Zane loved numbers and money, and had made Wall Street his hunting ground. Mav was a geek, despite not looking like a stereotypical one. He'd grown up in a strong, Mexican-American family, and with his brown skin, broad shoulders, and the fact that he worked out a lot, no one would pick him for a tech billionaire.

But under the big body, the man was a computer geek to the bone.

"All the society mamas are giving you lots of speculative looks." Mav gave him a small grin.

"Shut it, Rivera."

"They're all dreaming of marrying their daughters off to billionaire Zane Roth, the finance King of Wall Street."

Zane glared. "You done?"

"Oh, I could go on."

"I seem to recall another article about the billionaire bachelors. All three of us." Zane tipped his glass at his friend. "They'll be coming for you, next."

Mav's smile dissolved, and he shrugged a broad shoulder. "I'll toss Kensington at them. He's pretty."

Liam Kensington was the third member of their trio. Unlike Zane and Mav, Liam had come from money, although he worked hard to avoid his bloodsucking family.

Zane saw a woman in a slinky, blue dress shoot him a welcoming smile.

He looked away.

When he'd made his first billion, he'd welcomed the attention. Especially the female attention. He'd bedded more than his fair share of gorgeous women.

Of late, nothing and no one caught his interest. Women all left him feeling numb.

Work. He thrived on that.

A part of him figured he'd never find a woman who made him feel the same way as his work.

"Speak of the devil," Mav said.

Zane looked up to see Liam Kensington striding toward them. With the lean body of a swimmer, clad in a perfectly tailored tuxedo, he looked every inch the billionaire. His gold hair complemented a face the ladies oohed over.

People tried to get his attention, but the real estate mogul ignored everyone.

He reached Zane and Mav, grabbed Zane's wine, and emptied it in two gulps.

"I hate this party. When can we leave?" Having spent his formative years in London, he had a posh British accent. Another thing the ladies loved. "I have a contract to work on, my fundraiser ball to plan, and things to catch up on after our trip to San Francisco."

The three of them had just returned from a business trip to the West Coast.

"Can't leave until the auction's done," Zane said.

Liam sighed. His handsome face often had him voted the best-looking billionaire bachelor.

"Buy up big," Zane said. "Proceeds go to the Boys and Girls Clubs."

"One of your pet charities," Liam said.

"Yeah." Zane's father had left when he was seven. His mom had worked hard to support them. She was his hero. He liked to give back to charities that supported kids growing up in tough circumstances.

He'd set his mom up in a gorgeous house Upstate that she loved. And he was here for her tonight.

"Don't bid on the Phillips-Morley necklace, though," he added. "It's mine."

The necklace had a huge, rectangular sapphire pendant surrounded by diamonds. It was the real-life necklace said to have inspired the necklace in the movie, *Titanic*. It had been given to a young woman, Kate Florence Phillips, by her lover, Henry Samuel Morley. The two had run away together and booked passage on the Titanic.

Unfortunately for poor Kate, Henry had drowned when the ship had sunk. She'd returned to England with the necklace and a baby in her belly.

Zane's mother had always loved the story and pored over pictures of the necklace. She'd told him the story of the lovers, over and over.

"It was a gift from a man to a woman he loved. She was a shop girl, and he owned the store, but they fell in love, even though society frowned on their love." She sighed. "That's true love, Zane. Devotion, loyalty, through the good times and the bad."

Everything Carol Roth had never known.

Of course, it turned out old Henry was much older than his lover, and already married. But Zane didn't want to ruin the fairy tale for his mom.

Now, the Phillips-Morley necklace had turned up, and was being offered at auction. And Zane was going to get it for his mom. It was her birthday in a few months.

"Hey, is your fancy, new safe ready yet?" Zane asked Mav.

His friend nodded. "You're getting one of the first ones. I can have my team install it this week."

"Perfect." Mav's new Riv3000 was the latest in high-tech safes and said to be unbreakable. "I'll keep the necklace in it until my mom's birthday."

Someone called out Liam's name. With a sigh, their friend forced a smile. "Can't dodge this one. Simpson's an investor in my Brooklyn project. I'll be back."

"Need a refill?" Zane asked Mav.

"Sure."

Zane headed for the bar. He'd almost reached it when a manicured hand snagged his arm.

"Zane."

He looked down at the woman and barely swallowed his groan. "Allegra. You look lovely this evening."

She did. Allegra Montgomery's shimmery, silver dress hugged her slender figure, and her cloud of mahogany brown hair accented her beautiful face. As the only daughter of a wealthy New York family—her father was from *the* Montgomery family and her mother was a former Miss America—Allegra was well-bred and well-educated but also, as he'd discovered, spoiled and liked getting her way.

Her dark eyes bored into him. "I'm sorry things ended badly for us the other month. I was..." Her voice lowered, and she stroked his forearm. "I miss you. I was hoping we could catch up again."

Zane arched a brow. They'd dated for a few weeks, shared a few dinners, and some decent sex. But Allegra liked being the center of attention, complained that he worked too much, and had constantly hounded him to take her on vacation. Preferably on a private jet to Tahiti or the Maldives.

When she'd asked him if it would be too much for him to give her a credit card of her own, for monthly expenses, Zane had exited stage left.

"I don't think so, Allegra. We aren't...compatible."

Her full lips turned into a pout. "I thought we were *very* compatible."

He cleared his throat. "I heard you moved on. With Chip Huffington."

Allegra waved a hand. "Oh, that's nothing serious."

And Chip was only a millionaire. Allegra would see that as a step down. In fact, Zane felt like every time she looked at him, he could almost see little dollar signs in her eyes.

He dredged up a smile. "I wish you all the best, Allegra. Good evening." He sidestepped her and made a beeline for the bar.

"What can I get you?" the bartender asked.

Wine wasn't going to cut it. It would probably be frowned on to ask for an entire bottle of Scotch. "Two glasses of Scotch, please. On the rocks. Do you have Macallan?"

"No, sorry, sir. Will Glenfiddich do?"

"Sure."

"Ladies and gentlemen," a voice said over the loudspeaker. The lights lowered. "I hope you're ready to spend big for a wonderful cause."

Carrying the drinks, Zane hurried back to Mav and Liam. He handed Mav a glass.

"Let's do this," Mav grumbled. "And next time, I'll make a generous online donation so I don't have to come to the party."

"Drinks at my place after I get the necklace," Zane said. "I have a very good bottle of Macallan."

Mav stilled. "How good?"

"Macallan 25. Single malt."

"I'm there," Liam said.

Mav lifted his chin.

Ahead, Zane watched the evening's host lift a black cloth off a pedestal. He stared at the necklace, the sapphire glittering under the lights.

There it was.

The sapphire was a deep, rich blue. Just like all the photos his mother had shown him.

"Get that damn necklace, Roth, and let's get out of here," Mav said.

Zane nodded. He'd get the necklace for the one woman in his life who rarely asked for anything, then escape the rest of the bloodsuckers and hang with his friends.

Billionaire Heists
Stealing from Mr. Rich
Blackmailing Mr. Bossman
Hacking Mr. CEO

W ant to learn more about the mysterious, covert *Team 52*? Check out the first book in the series, *Mission: Her Protection.*

When Rowan's Arctic research team pulls a strange object out of the ice in Northern

Canada, things start to go wrong...very, very wrong. Rescued by a covert, black ops team, she finds herself in the powerful arms of a man with scary gold eyes. A man who vows to do everything and anything to protect her...

Dr. Rowan Schafer has learned it's best to do things herself and not depend on anyone else. Her cold, academic parents taught her that lesson. She loves the challenge of running a research base, until the day her scientists discover the object in a retreating glacier. Under attack, Rowan finds herself fighting to survive... until the mysterious Team 52 arrives.

Former special forces Marine Lachlan Hunter's military career ended in blood and screams, until he was recruited to lead a special team. A team tasked with a top-secret mission—to secure and safeguard pieces of powerful ancient technology. Married to his job, he's done too much and seen too much to risk inflicting his demons on a woman. But when his team arrives in the Arctic, he uncovers both an unexplained artifact, and a young girl from his past, now all grown up. A woman who ignites emotions inside him like never before.

But as Team 52 heads back to their base in Nevada, other hostile forces are after the artifact. Rowan finds herself under attack, and as the bullets fly, Lachlan vows to protect her at all costs. But in the face of danger like they've never seen before, will it be enough to keep her alive.

Team 52
Mission: Her Protection
Mission: Her Rescue
Mission: Her Security
Mission: Her Defense
Mission: Her Safety
Mission: Her Freedom
Mission: Her Shield
Also Available as Audiobooks!

Want to learn more about *Treasure Hunter Security*? Check out the first book in the series, *Undiscovered*, Declan Ward's action-packed story.

One former Navy SEAL. One dedicated archeologist. One secret map to a fabulous lost oasis.

Finding undiscovered treasures is always daring, dangerous, and deadly. Perfect for the men of Treasure Hunter Security. Former Navy SEAL Declan Ward is haunted by the demons of his past and throws everything he has into his security business—Treasure Hunter Security. Dangerous archeological digs – no problem. Daring expeditions – sure thing. Museum security for invaluable exhibits – easy. But on a simple dig in the Egyptian desert, he collides with a stubborn, smart archeologist, Dr. Layne Rush, and together they get swept into a deadly treasure hunt for a mythical lost oasis. When an evil from his past reappears, Declan vows to do anything to protect Layne.

Dr. Layne Rush is dedicated to building a successful career—a promise to the parents she lost far too young. But when her dig is plagued by strange accidents, targeted by a lethal black market antiquities ring, and artifacts are stolen, she is forced to turn to Treasure Hunter Security, and to the tough, sexy, and too-used-to-giving-orders Declan. Soon her organized dig morphs into a wild treasure hunt across the desert dunes.

Danger is hunting them every step of the way, and Layne and Declan must find a way to work together...to not only find the treasure but to survive.

Treasure Hunter Security
Undiscovered
Uncharted
Unexplored
Unfathomed

Untraveled
Unmapped
Unidentified
Undetected
Also Available as Audiobooks!

ALSO BY ANNA HACKETT

Norcross Security

The Investigator

The Troubleshooter

The Specialist

The Bodyguard

The Hacker

Billionaire Heists

Stealing from Mr. Rich

Blackmailing Mr. Bossman

Hacking Mr. CEO

Team 52

Mission: Her Protection

Mission: Her Rescue

Mission: Her Security

Mission: Her Defense

Mission: Her Safety

Mission: Her Freedom

Mission: Her Shield

Mission: Her Justice

Also Available as Audiobooks!

Treasure Hunter Security

Undiscovered

Uncharted

Unexplored

Unfathomed

Untraveled

Unmapped

Unidentified

Undetected

Also Available as Audiobooks!

Eon Warriors

Edge of Eon

Touch of Eon

Heart of Eon

Kiss of Eon

Mark of Eon

Claim of Eon

Storm of Eon

Soul of Eon

King of Eon

Also Available as Audiobooks!

Galactic Gladiators: House of Rone

Sentinel

Defender

Centurion

Paladin

Guard

Weapons Master

Also Available as Audiobooks!

Galactic Gladiators

Gladiator

Warrior

Hero

Protector

Champion

Barbarian

Beast

Rogue

Guardian

Cyborg

Imperator

Hunter

Also Available as Audiobooks!

Hell Squad

Marcus

Cruz

Gabe

Reed

Roth

Noah

Shaw

Holmes

Niko

Finn

Devlin

Theron

Hemi

Ash

Levi

Manu

Griff

Dom

Survivors

Tane

Also Available as Audiobooks!

The Anomaly Series

Time Thief

Mind Raider

Soul Stealer

Salvation

Anomaly Series Box Set

The Phoenix Adventures

Among Galactic Ruins

At Star's End

In the Devil's Nebula

On a Rogue Planet

Beneath a Trojan Moon

Beyond Galaxy's Edge

On a Cyborg Planet

Return to Dark Earth

On a Barbarian World

Lost in Barbarian Space

Through Uncharted Space

Crashed on an Ice World

Perma Series

Winter Fusion

A Galactic Holiday

Warriors of the Wind

Tempest

Storm & Seduction

Fury & Darkness

Standalone Titles

Savage Dragon

Hunter's Surrender

One Night with the Wolf

For more information visit www.annahackett.com

ABOUT THE AUTHOR

I'm a USA Today bestselling romance author who's passionate about **_fast-paced, emotion-filled_** contemporary romantic suspense and science fiction romance. I love writing about people overcoming unbeatable odds and achieving seemingly impossible goals. I like to believe it's possible for all of us to do the same.

I live in Australia with my own personal hero and two very busy, always-on-the-move sons.

For release dates, behind-the-scenes info, free books, and other fun stuff, sign up for the latest news here:

Website: www.annahackett.com

Made in the USA
Las Vegas, NV
06 November 2021